WAKE

WAKE

Stories

Beth Goldner

COUNTERPOINT

ISBN: 978-1-58243-269-4

Library of Congress Cataloging-in-Publication Data

Goldner, Beth.
    Wake : stories / Beth Goldner.
        p. cm.
    ISBN 1-58243-269-4 (alk. paper)
    1. Psychological fiction, American. 2. Loss (Psychology)--Fiction. I. Title.

PS3607.O46W35 2003
813'.6--dc21

                                                        2003006392

The following stories have been previously published, some of them in a slightly different form: "Farm Wife" appeared in *Literal Latté* (April 2001); "Plan B" appeared in the *Massachusetts Review* (winter 2000–2001); "Outcomes" appeared in the *Blue Mesa Review* (2001); "Waxing" appeared in *Story Quarterly* (fall 2002).

Very special thanks to my agent, Noah Lukeman, for making this happen. Thanks also to the staff at Counterpoint, especially Dawn Seferian, Sarah McNally, and Rebecca Marks. These stories were read in their early drafts by good friends, and I thank them for their support and encouragement, especially Chris, Tanya, Sharon, and Ken. Finally, thanks to Susan for her technical expertise, to MaryAnn for helping me see the possibilities, to Megan for being the first muse, and to Amy, Jane, and Carol for years of priceless one-liners.

For Linda, Juli, and Debra

CONTENTS

WAKE   1

TAXI DANCER   25

CARDIFF-BY-THE-SEA   51

EXPATRIATES   67

WAXING   85

FARM WIFE   107

PLAN B   123

OUTCOMES   139

CHECKMATE   161

DEEP DOWN TO THE BOTTOM OF THIS   179

BAD ASS BOB, A MUG SHOT MUG, A MAN   201

WAKE

WAKE

IN THE AUTUMN OF 1979, my sister Jill insisted that we make funeral plans for Munk, our black-and-white calico cat. At the time, Munk was neither sick nor old.

I was ten years old, Jill was twelve, and for months our parents had been playing a version of musical chairs at the psychiatric ward of Pennsylvania Hospital. First our dad went in for a few weeks. Then he came out. Then our mom went in for a few weeks. Then she came out. In and out and back and forth and running in circles, they both tried to seize the unoccupied chair.

The day Jill announced that a trial-run funeral for Munk was needed, our mother arrived home from a three-week stay at the hospital. I remember seeing her standing on the front porch as our father took her suitcase from the backseat of our faux-wood paneled station wagon. All of us—Jill, our two older sisters, Nora and Sally, and myself—huddled telepathically, wondering how long it would take for our dad to plant himself in the open chair. Technically speaking, it was his turn. But seven hours after our mother's discharge that overcast Saturday, she thwarted him: her unpacked suitcase was brought downstairs, and our father drove her back to the hospital.

"Munk needs to be in the funeral, of course," Jill said, "but I don't think she'll sit still long enough."

"Maybe we should use a stuffed animal in Munk's place," I suggested.

"That's not real enough," Jill said. "It needs to feel real."

I quietly watched Jill. She would come up with something: Jill was an ideas person. She had hair the color of cherry wood, hazel eyes with pinpricks of gold, was skinny as blades of grass, and it seemed as if all fires of hell flamed through her. She was raging that autumn, simply raging, with fear more than anything, because fear runs deep when you're tucked away in a four-bedroom split-level on a quiet street and your father, not coming out of his room, is silenced by a darkness that only the depths of oceans know. And your mother is in the psychiatric ward again, agoraphobic and so profoundly sad with an unnamable sadness. And since Jill had to get her hands around something—we couldn't wrap our hands around much that autumn—she was going to aim high. She was going to go bigger and better and darker than just two clinically ill parents and a home that few others aside from its faithful inhabitants knew was so terribly strangled in pain and brokenness. Jill was going to wrap her hands around Death.

"I know," Jill said, a ray of clarity in her eyes, "we'll make a sculpture of Munk. That's what we'll do. We'll make a sculpture of Munk, and we can have a wake and a funeral. And we'll invite Kimmy, Pam, and Sharon over and they can be the mourners."

Kimmy, Pam, and Sharon Peterson were three sisters close in age to Jill and me who lived on our block. The Petersons were devout Christians. They were so Christian they weren't allowed to ride their bikes on Sunday.

"Do we know how to make a sculpture?" I asked Jill.

"No. But we can figure it out," she said.

"Well, who is going to be the priest?"

"I will, of course," Jill snapped.

"What will I be?"

"A pallbearer," she promptly replied, and she walked off to find some paper and a pencil. First she was going make a sketch of what the dead cat sculpture would look like. She wanted to draw it out.

This is what I could not know then, when Jill made plans for a funeral for our very-much-alive cat: That three years later, I'd go to a concert at JFK Stadium in Philadelphia with my stepsister, Rita, to see The Who. I did not know then that I would even have a stepsister. That I would smoke pot for the first time and be frightened by it, how all the people—100,000 of us—were crammed in the outdoor stadium, how the crowd looked like waves of worms struggling against the hot sun. That I would run into my sister Jill at the concert, in that big crowd, the smallest chance, the fate of it all—to run into Jill, who lived with our father.

This is what I could not know: That when our parents finally stopped playing musical chairs, the music would stop altogether, and the players would separate. That in the wake of their separation and divorce came the end of me and Jill sharing a room, sharing a life. She went to live with our father; I stayed with our mother. Nora and Sally left altogether. Nora went to college in upstate New York. Sally joined the Army and was stationed 1,500 miles away in Alabama. Jill and I were the only ones left in the rhythmic movement of our parents' demise. And this was not tragedy, this was not hardship when you really think of hardship in the grand scheme of burning disasters and long slow deaths and painful cancers that rip through nerve endings, and flies in the eyes of starving children in Africa with bloated bellies and just no hope at all. This was not tragedy, but it was our march.

Santana was on stage. But it was The Who that Jill and I were waiting for, each of us not knowing how close we were, how we arrived separately, not knowing the other was there, wanting the same thing. We both wanted Roger Daltrey and his sinewy chest and perfectly cut arms and the way he screamed into the microphone. We wanted Pete Townshend, his arm swinging in circles, working genius with his guitar.

I could hear Carlos Santana's guitar in the background as I stood alone in a long line for the bathroom. I had left Rita and her boyfriend, Bruce, back at our seats, where stoned and in love, they kissed and groped, oblivious to the music and the crowds and me. And then there she was: Jill and her best friend, Melissa, in line about ten people behind me. Jill was wearing cutoff blue jeans and a black tee shirt that said *The Who Farewell Tour 1982,* which she must have bought from a vendor only hours earlier. I didn't even shout her name. I just screamed. Like my guts were bursting. I screamed and my throat was sore and smoky and scratchy. And when I screamed, Jill turned her head and looked right at me. She didn't say my name either. She just screamed.

We lost our places in that long line; we just gave them up, ran and entwined arms around each other, jumped up and down and screamed. Because here she was, my sister Jill, who I shared a bedroom with for the first 11 years of my life, who in the last two years had become someone I'd see only on Wednesday nights for dinner and every other weekend when I went to the apartment on Northrop Street in Wallingford where she lived with our dad. My sister Jill, who had the same superball-at-the-tip bulbous nose as me, who when I was six years old paid me a nickel to pee in my slipper, who beat me up, who stole our mom's cigarettes, who wrote to Jimmy Carter and got an autographed picture of him that she would let me look at sometimes.

"I can't believe Mom let you come here," she shouted. "Who the fuck are you here with?"

"Rita," I said, switching from screaming to laughing.

Laughing because I was with our stepsister, Rita, who didn't even have to go to school. Our mom and stepfather did not make Rita go to school because she had already run away once, somehow getting from Pennsylvania to Minneapolis. Months after she ran away, she was found, and our mom and stepfather knew if they tried to make her do what she didn't want to do, she would run away again. So instead of going to high school, Rita made bacon-cheese-and-onion hamburgers at Wendy's Restaurant. She wore a brown polyester uniform that smelled like meat no matter how much she washed it, and she stole money from the cash register without getting caught. Rita would come home at night with odd amounts of stolen money: $17.48, $22.43, $13.52. She'd take the money she earned and the money she stole, and she bought makeup, cigarettes, pot, and albums, and she'd get stoned every night, sneak Bruce into her room through her bedroom window (he was lanky and like a monkey, scaling the drain post to get to the second floor roof), and then she would spend the rest of the night having sex with him.

"You're here with Rita? Figures. Just absolutely fucking figures," Jill said, shaking her head in disbelief.

This is the one thing I did know then and there at that Who concert: That Jill hated Rita. And that Rita hated Jill. The venom of their hatred. That on the afternoon our mother married Rita's father, during the small and modest reception held at our house, Jill and Rita's boyfriend, Bruce, sucked face behind the shed in the backyard, the same shed that we held Munk's wake in.

～♏～

It rained the afternoon Jill finished drawing on paper what a dead cat sculpture would look like. After the rain stopped, Jill and I went to the backyard, behind the shed where there was a small patch of dirt that served as a tomato garden every summer. Jill decided that the sculpture of Munk would be made of mud. *Mud dries and hardens,* she pointed out. We had no clay. But we had mud.

The dirt was wet and sticky and full of stones and rocks. *It's perfect,* Jill said, *how the rocks help hold the sculpture together.* It had been three days since our mother pulled her check-out-and-check-back-in to Pennsylvania Hospital. And in another three days our dad would drive us four sisters, his brood of daughters, to the hospital to visit her. For in three days, it would be our mother's birthday.

This is what I knew then, while in the garden with my hands deep in the mud: That I had to make my mother a birthday gift. Because when you have your 38th birthday in a psychiatric ward and you are so out of it that it could be your 28th or your 48th birthday and you wouldn't know the difference, and your equally out-of-it husband is at home waiting for his turn in the chair, and you have four daughters you love but you just don't have the energy to deal with, well, it's the kind of birthday where gifts mean nothing at all, and yet you need them more than ever.

I had no money to buy her a gift, because when your parents take turns going in and out, the swaying motion of that, allowance falls by the wayside. You just don't bother asking for things like allowance and violin lessons and for the showing up needed, like a ride to Leanne Klausner's house for a sleepover party. You don't ask for someone to take you to Woolworth's to buy your mother a bottle of Jean Naté perfume or a mug that says *World's Best Mom*. There are less ordinary things to be dealt with. So you know you will make a gift. You know you will just have to make it.

I decided to make my mother a shoe box diorama. I had recently made one for a fifth-grade project in which we had to highlight an important historical event; I chose the sinking of the *PT 109*. On August 2, 1943, a young John F. Kennedy was at the helm of the *PT 109*, patrolling the Pacific Ocean to intercept Japanese warships near the Ferguson and Blackett Straits. I showcased the incident in a Kinney's Shoes shoe box that originally housed a pair of caramel-brown sling-back wedges of my mother's: How JFK's boat was severed in half by the Japanese destroyer *Amagiri*. How the crash threw him onto the floor of the ship, injuring his already bad back. How there, in the wrestling waters of the Solomon Islands, JFK led his surviving crew to swim from island to island, where they found no inhabitants. How he then led them to swim to Olasana Island, where some natives discovered them. How Kennedy scratched an SOS message on a coconut and gave it to the natives to take to Rendova Island, where the American PT base was situated.

It seemed so improbable, so extraordinary, to be faced with a sinking ship and a bad back and an injured crew, swimming from one island to the next trying to figure out how to make it work. The *PT 109* shoe box diorama was not a pivotal historical event to my fellow classmates. But nevertheless it was chosen by my teacher, Mrs. Hayes, for the coveted glass display in the back of the classroom. It was chosen because she knew about the drama—not in JFK's military years but in my household.

Mrs. Hayes was a white woman who happened to be married to a black man. I remember her standing there on the first day of school, facing a brightly lit roomful of ten-year-olds. She was pale, with a head of dark red curly hair. She slowly and intentionally swayed back and forth on her feet, heel to toe, toe to heel, her hands swinging behind her for a clap and then in front of her for a clap, back and forth, clap and clap, and then she said her first words to us: "My name is Caroline Hayes. I'm 36 years old. And I'm married to a black man. Any questions?"

In our rock-solid-white suburban enclave, Mrs. Hayes's holy matrimony with a black man left her disenfranchised and thus sympathetic, I was convinced, to my own version of disenfranchisement. She chose my diorama because she knew what was happening in my house. She chose my diorama because I had no questions (none of us did that day when she clapped and spoke), and I certainly had no answers.

"I can't believe Mrs. Hayes chose your diorama," Jacob Adler said to me. Jacob was an intense ten-year-old who was drunk with knowledge of history, particularly war history. He could detail the particulars of the Treaty of Versailles, tell you the exact path Hitler took in seizing Europe, and he could tell you exactly how many wounded soldiers passed through Malta's military hospital, the largest in the Mediterranean, during the First World War. For the diorama project, Jacob had created a frighteningly realistic and accurate rendition of the bombing of Hiroshima.

"I mean, who cares that some President's boat collided with a bunch of Japs?" Jacob continued, bits of frustrated spit coming out of his mouth.

"It was a serious military situation that showed Kennedy's true courage," I said in a barely audible voice.

"We bombed the hell out of those Japs and won the war. Now that matters," Jacob snorted.

"But courage matters. And John Kennedy was only, like, 26 years old when this happened," I continued, defending what little I had to cling to.

"Yeah, so what," Jacob replied, "Did you know that some Kamikaze pilots were only 17? Think about it—17 years old. Now that's courage."

This is what I could not know then: That as a 17-year-old I would covet Katie Barzansky's life. I would covet her life because her boyfriend was Jacob. And I wanted Jacob. I didn't care about courage then. I didn't need or want courage. What I wanted was Jacob's mouth. I wanted my mouth on his. I wanted to taste him. I could not know then that as a 33-year-old I would hear from friends who showed up to our 15-year high school reunion that Jacob was gay. That he was there with his Portuguese lover, Eduardo. That Jacob's hair was dyed blond. That his lover was 21.

For my mother's birthday diorama, I used a Florsheim Shoes shoe box that originally held a pair of our father's dark brown loafers, shoes that our father rarely wore. He was an aeronautical engineer who designed discrete parts for airplanes, and he worked in a laboratory building things with other engineers—combustion engineers and jet propulsion engineers and structural engineers—so his shoe of choice was a black work boot with reinforced steel tips.

The scene for my mother's birthday diorama was simple: Our backyard. The back of the house, our grass greener than it really was, the tulip tree that every summer would sprout an orange and yellow flower toward its top, the tomato garden with tomatoes, ripe and full, in mass quantity, red heavy fruit falling off the vine.

This is what I did not know then: That many months after I gave our mother this shoe box diorama, when our father had left (Jill would follow not even three months later to live with him), that I would go rummaging in the closet of our parent's bedroom looking for something—wrapping paper, an ironing board, whatever—and I would find the diorama buried under crap and junk and old shoes and clothes that needed to go to Salvation Army, shoved way under this ridiculous pile of things that had no meaning or value but that could not be thrown away.

This is what I could not know, not when I was 10, not when I was 13: That when Jill was 30 and I was 28, she would have a mole removed.

It was a mole all four of us sisters had, each in the same place. Nora and Sally already had their mole removed for the same reason Jill eventually would—location. Our mole was under the right breast, just precisely where the most underside of the breast meets the first rib. A brown, simple, small raised mole. When making love, it would peak out if you were flat on your back. When you were standing up naked, with your arms flat down against your side, the mole was hidden.

All of us grew breasts of various sizes—Nora a C cup, Sally and Jill a B cup, and me, a meager A. My mole was visible most of the time because of my small breasts. I could not know that the mole would become part of us, a signature of ourselves, of our sisterhood: hidden, then removed.

Nora had her mole removed first, tired of it being rubbed by her underwire bra. The pathology report on its cellular nature would be fine. A few years later Sally got her mole removed. The cells were normal; all was ordinary. But then she mentioned the mole to Nora, who laughed about having the same mole removed, and then they told Jill and me, and then we all discovered we were the same, exactly the same, in this small way. Years later, Jill would have hers cut off. But when Jill's was taken off, the sameness ended. Because Jill's mole, according to the pathology report, was atypical.

"Everything about you is atypical," I said, trying to make a joke, for both of our sakes, "I wouldn't worry about it."

But then they cut more. They dug deeper with sharper knives. More pathology reports. More cellular levels. More information: Jill was not the same.

I was still undaunted, holding onto my mole. My boyfriend, Aaron, was fascinated by it, ran his tongue across it every time we made love. He named it Clara. Aaron was the first man to make me come and he loved my mole, and I was scared of jinxing it right then and there. I wanted to keep everything in its place, the man I loved, the sisters I had, the mole under my right breast.

And when they cut more under Jill's breast, her translucent and opaque skin, bluish and clear like skim milk, they cut deep and wide and stitched her up with thick and wiry thread.

Jill was quick to start the base of the dead cat sculpture, but I was lulled into a trance by the way the little rocks in the mud felt on my hands, how the rough edges were softened by the wet dirt. Jill got a wooden plank from the shed and we worked. We shaped and created. Hands covered in brown and touching, we molded a dead cat out of mud.

"You know, the Irish came up with the idea of a wake," Jill said.

"I don't even know what a wake is," I confessed.

"A wake is the Irish version of a viewing, but it's not at the funeral parlor. It's at the dead person's house. The family puts the dead person on the kitchen table, and then for three days everyone the dead person knew comes over and eats and drinks around the kitchen table and talks about all the good times they had with the dead person."

"You can't put a dead person on a kitchen table," I said.

"You sure can. Nowadays the dead person is in a casket, but the most important part, with or without a casket, is that they are on the kitchen table."

"I don't think Dad is going to let us put the sculpture of Munk on the kitchen table for three days," I said.

"Dad wouldn't notice if Munk's sculpture was on the kitchen table for three weeks."

I paused.

"Well, I don't think Nora and Sally will let us," I said.

Jill paused. We both knew this was true. Nora and Sally were in charge. They made special arrangements with the high school so that they did not have a first-period class. This allowed them to wake us up, to make sure that we got our fill of sugary Fruit Loops, that made our milk turn pastel colors, that we would begin our walk to school, a walk in a neighborhood where oak trees were young, a neighborhood where people fought with silence and in silence. It didn't matter who was in the hospital at the time—our older sisters were on duty. We had to listen to Nora and Sally, who were forced to care for us and feed us and resent us and then pack up their books and go to school, to their second-period class, to be normal, to be pimply and wear platform shoes and wonder if they would have a prom date so they could buy that maroon tie-dye dress that sunk low in the cleavage and then spend the night with everyone at the Jersey Shore and have sex on the beach. They had to do both—be teenagers and be parents. And as parents,

Jill and I knew they would not tolerate a mud sculpture of Munk on the kitchen table for a three-day wake.

"We'll just have a one-day wake then. We're German, and quite frankly, Germans know how to get to the point. The Irish tend to take too long with things. And we'll put Munk's sculpture in the shed, on the tool chest. It's not a kitchen table, but it's close enough."

Jill came over to my apartment the evening after the doctor took the second cut of flesh from where the mole had been. She came bounding in, threw her purse on the floor and then hoisted her shirt up and stripped it right off.

"Look," she said, stridently crossing the room, almost excited.

She didn't unhook her bra, but lifted it gingerly, wincing as she did.

"Look at it," she said, peeling back the heavy gauze bandage, showing me the two-inch-long cut that was gripped together by thick black stitches whose ends shot out like thin legs.

"It looks like a spider," I said.

"Yeah," she said, looking down at it, "it does. I hate spiders."

I let her take my hand and bring it to her skin and touch the wiry spider of thread.

There had been a spider in my house that evening before Jill arrived. I had spent an hour trying to figure out how to kill it. Despite the fact that it rested contentedly on a web it had built on my living room window, I was convinced the spider was planning to catch me off guard and move quickly from its web to my leg. I called Aaron for assistance.

"Just get a magazine and give it a good whack," Aaron said to me over the phone.

"But it's so big."

"It's not going to jump you or anything," he said.

"How do you know that?"

"Because, well—hello there—it's a fucking spider," he said, frustrated.

This is what I could not know then: That his frustrations would continue. That Aaron would fail every time I was distressed or under pressure or emotional. He would fail every time I really needed him. That when Jill's spider crawled through her, when I would come home from visiting her and feel guilty and confused by my steady, seamlessly functioning body and overcome with sadness, that Aaron would be unable to deal with his healthy thriving lover. I could not know then that he could not handle the insects that crawl through our lives and make us squirm.

"I can't just kill it with a magazine because it will know I am coming after it and it will jump on me first," I said.

"And just how will the spider know all of this?"

"Things this big have thoughts," I stated firmly.

I watched the spider for a long time, and then I sprayed Windex on it until it fell to the floor. Then I slammed the 27th edition of *Dorland's Illustrated Medical Dictionary*, which I had found for 25 cents at a garage sale, on top of it. Then I stood on top of the dictionary, which was on the Windex-coated spider, and I jumped up and down. And I kept jumping for a while. I wanted to make sure it was dead, that it was really gone.

This is what I could not know: That killing spiders really truly is bad luck. That the spider under my sister's breast was just the tip of the iceberg that would keep getting dug out and cut, an iceberg tip that was not just atypical but that the next report would call malignant. That the iceberg would weave a web throughout her insides and glands and nodes. That I would be 30 years old and still have my mole but not have my sister.

On the day of Munk's wake, also our mother's birthday, I stood in my and Jill's bedroom staring at the mud sculpture of Munk. It looked remarkably well considering the materials we had. The dead cat sculpture was in the sphinx position—flat on the belly, back legs tucked under, front legs out forward and parallel, head held high. I considered presenting the dead cat sculpture to our mother instead of the shoe box diorama I had made. Munk frequently brought dead animals to our doorstep. Our father said these offerings of dead cardinals in rigor mortis and eviscerated mice were considered a sign of love and faithfulness.

At the hospital, when I handed my mother the shoe box diorama, she opened it with slow-moving hands, barely looked at it, and then put it in the pile next to all the other gifts she didn't really care about. I did not know what she cared about. I just wanted her to care.

"They should give her shock treatments like they gave Dad," my sister Nora said later when we got home. "At least she'd seem a bit more awake."

The four of us were all in the kitchen. Our father had already gone upstairs into our parent's bedroom, where he would stay for the next several hours.

"She seemed awake," I said, because I felt like I had to say something.

"Give me a fucking break," Jill said to me.

"Watch your mouth," Nora and Sally barked simultaneously.

"You," Jill said pointing her finger at Nora, "and you," pointing at Sally, "cannot tell me what to do. You are not my mother."

"Thank God for that," Nora sighed.

Our front doorbell rang and Nora went to answer it. I knew it was the Peterson sisters, here for the wake.

"The holy roller sisters are here," Nora said, walking back in the kitchen. "They're waiting for you on the porch."

The Peterson sisters rarely came inside our house. They were always invited, but only on a few occasions would they come in. Instead, they would wait on the porch, and then we'd come out to play. In foul weather, we'd play in our shed or inside their house. The Peterson sisters were our friends, but it was a friendship forged by the default nature of tract-housing communities during the 1970s: You didn't choose your friends, you just became friends with whoever lived on your street. So we went inside their house and they didn't come in ours; these were simply the terms of our relationship.

The five of us crammed into the rusting blue shed, where Jill had already moved the dead cat sculpture. We huddled close, surrounded by rakes and tools and brooms. Jill announced that the wake would be opened with a prayer. The Peterson sisters looked solemn. They prayed in their house all the time, before every meal, even if it was only a lunch of peanut butter and jelly sandwiches and celery sticks.

"Heavenly Father," Jill said, standing behind the sculpture with her eyes shut and her head back and her hands folded together pressed against her chest, "we bequeath You to bless the passing of our dearly beloved cat, Munk."

"Beseech," Pam, the oldest Peterson sister, whispered suddenly.

"What?" Jill hissed back, annoyed.

"Beseech. Not bequeath. You beseech the Lord," Pam replied with the confidence of a girl who knew her Scriptures.

"Lord," Jill continued, "we beseech you to bring our dearly departed Munk into your heavenly gates," Jill said, exaggerating *beseech*, looking Pam Peterson right in the eye, showing all of us who was at the helm of the ritual of death.

"Let the wake begin," Jill said as her head rose and her arms lowered.

We stood there, the five of us, staring at the dead cat sculpture, not knowing what to say or do. Jill stood proudly, smiling, and it didn't matter that we didn't know what to do. Because to Jill, we were already doing it. We just needed to be there. That was all. As we stood there, the live version of that which we worshipped slithered into the shed. Our cat could not resist a crowd, and she walked right in and opened her mouth, crying to us.

This is what I could not know: That sadness is not always extraordinary. I was convinced that autumn our parents circled the chairs that I would always know extraordinary sadness, that the hugeness of it would carry on throughout my life, but I did not know that the sadness would cycle, would leave and then come back in different ways, with people coming out of their darkness, and others entering into new dark places.

That all that was the history of my youth would be wrapped in small black-and-white picture slides: the four of us in winter coats standing against the brick side of our house; standing in the backyard by the tulip tree; Nora standing on the front porch in her white First Holy Communion dress in shiny black patent leather shoes and a big scab on her knee. The slides were from pictures our father had taken before the musical chairs and the divorce. Jill and I used to view them with the slide projector that had a handheld clicker. The slides were salvaged from the garbage pile in front of the house near the mailbox, salvaged by Nora. After the divorce, our mother put the slides in a big green plastic garbage bag and, in the darkness of a Monday evening, put them out by the garbage. (No one was supposed to see this but Nora saw. Nora saw her throwing them in the bag and then marching them outside into the rainy evening for a Tuesday morning pickup.) Nora snuck outside late that night and took the wet bag—which was sealed well— and Nora stole back our history. Nora took our history, put it in the trunk of her fading yellow 1970 Dodge Dart and, years later, after Jill's funeral, she divided up the slides.

I could not know that I would simplify, take the pain down a notch, even when it was Jill whom I stood wake for. It was really a viewing, but I kept calling it a wake, annoying Nora and Sally, who just didn't understand why I kept saying *wake* instead of *viewing*, who drenched by their own sadness were quick to lose their temper—we all were—our 32-year-old sister was dead and I couldn't stop saying that word. *Wake*, I said. That I would see all of this as ordinary, that the pain I held in my hands, clenched tight in fists to keep it from leaking out the seams between my fingers, that I would be scared to let it go, to let my fingers outstretch. I clung to the richness in pain, that pain with others, pain shared with sisters who annoy us and ignore us and move away from us and die—well, this is deep and rich, and without this pain, the loneliness in your heart (we all have it) is unbearable.

I could not know that I would believe in God—steadfast, assuredly believe in God—and in my inability to find courage. That I would hold onto the mole and tell everyone who knew about it that it was gone and removed and all was fine. And they never doubted it. Why would they? Who would ever keep the mole after all the moles and a sister were gone? Who would ever cling to something as strange and ambiguous and dark and unknown as that mole?

That I would lie in bed at night, weak, lonely, numbed— quite ordinary—and I would take my hand and move it down my breast, right to the underside, and touch the unknown, the mole, raised and small and mine.

Jill and I were lying in our twin beds, which were parallel and about a foot apart. Sometimes in the morning when we woke up, we wouldn't get out of bed right away. We would lie there and talk to each other before the day began, before she would start bossing me around, before seeing what kind of mood everyone was in and who had made it downstairs. At night, lying there, we'd talk again before going to sleep. And every once in a while she would stretch out her left arm and I would stretch out my right arm and we would hold hands.

"Do you know why they call a wake a wake?" Jill asked me. Munk's wake, brief and uneventful, was a success in Jill's eyes. Today was the funeral service.

"No," I said, "do you?"

"They call a wake a wake because about 100 years ago, sometimes a dead person wasn't really dead. They would be in a coma or just breathing shallow, so shallow that even the doctor thought they were dead. So there would be a wake not just to honor and celebrate the life of the dead person on the kitchen table but also just in case the person wasn't really dead and just needed some time to wake up. Get it? A wake. Just in case they would *wake* up."

"Is that for real?"

"Sure is."

"Who told you that?"

"Ronan. He's in my class. He's from Ireland, so he has firsthand information on these things," Jill said.

"So you're saying in some cases the person just seemed dead, but really wasn't?"

"Exactly," Jill said, and she got out of bed.

The funeral was going to be spectacular. That was the exact word Jill used as we sat there at the kitchen table eating breakfast. Our father was at Mass. We didn't have to go church during the time of musical chairs. It was another ordinary thing that just fell off the list of requirements. Nora and Sally were still sleeping.

The funeral was scheduled for noon. The Petersons, back from church by then and meticulous about time, arrived at

11:58. As long as we weren't riding bikes, they were allowed over on a Sunday to play. Jill led the five of us to the backyard to begin preparations. Jill and Pam began putting the red-and-white plastic lawn chairs under the tulip tree for the service. Jill thought the funeral should be held outside. *Munk's always been more of an outdoor than an indoor cat,* she pointed out. Jill brought the plank with the dead cat sculpture and placed it on a small table she had set up under the tulip tree. Then she placed small votive candles, which she had taken from the dining room hutch, around the dead cat sculpture. She draped a white sheet around her shoulders, aiming for a papal look. We were all excited. This was exciting. We wanted to honor a dark moment that we hadn't yet experienced.

Nora came outside just as the Peterson sisters seated themselves in the lawn chairs. She walked slowly toward us, her long blond hair pulled back loosely, her head hung strangely low. She told us in a quiet voice that we were invited to go have ice cream with the Schroeders. Paul and Kelly Schroeder were a young couple that lived four houses down, and Jill and I were frequently at their house. They never asked us about what was going on in our lives, but they always seemed glad to see us and they let us follow them around like needy dogs.

"The Schroeders will be by in a few minutes to get you guys," Nora said, failing to notice the scene under the tulip tree—the emergency candles around a dead cat mud sculpture, the sheets draped around Jill. Nora looked nervous. And Nora never looked nervous.

"All of us?" Jill asked.

"All five of you. That is, if the three of you are allowed," she said, addressing Pam.

"I'll go ask our parents," Pam said, running off to her house.

And so we all went, the five of us, for something special, for a treat, to have ice cream at Friendly's Family Restaurant. We dropped all that we were doing under the tulip tree, and Jill didn't fight it. She didn't hem or haw or moan about what she wanted to do right then and there, about the need to practice for a funeral. I don't know if it was the look in Nora's eye, if it was a sixth sense, or if it was just the mood Jill was in that day, but Jill let her idea be put aside. She let the plans change.

This is what we could not know then, while we ate ice cream with the Peterson sisters and Paul and Kelly Schroeder: That Nora and Sally were taking our father to the hospital. That our father, upon returning home from Mass, realized he could go no farther. That waiting for his turn in the chair would not do. That the pain that plagued him was not abated even slightly by parental necessity or the rules of the musical chair game.

We could not know this while eating ice cream with our neighbors, neighbors we didn't choose but neighbors that were ours. Jill had cherry vanilla ice cream. I had mint chocolate chip. We could not know that Nora had asked the Schroeder's to help with this, that our dad did not want Jill and I to see this, to see him coming down the stairs crying, with a suitcase, with no hope in that house, to see the new rule: No empty chair and still a parent could sit down. There were still some things we could not see.

We could not know that later that evening we would put the lawn chairs back in the shed, put the sheets away, cancel the funeral for a dead cat mud sculpture. It would be something to do another time. Later we could bury it.

TAXI DANCER

B OB AND I DON'T FUCK. We don't kiss or fondle or pet or caress. We dance. Which is how we met.

I'm a taxi dancer. I work at the Come-N-Go Retro Lounge. I live in Los Angeles with my boyfriend, Trevor, who spends his days doing bong hits and his nights waiting tables at an expensive French restaurant. Even though Trevor and I are living together, we are on a relationship hiatus while I'm in Europe for the summer. We're reevaluating. We're giving each other space. We're figuring out, each on our own, what we want to do. Whether we want to keep going or end it. Three months of me in Europe is a lot of space to think about how much space I may have when I get home.

Taxi dancing is easy. All you have to do is dance with your client. The lounge gets 20 percent of your take-in and you get a room to dance in. I set up a record player in the corner of the room. The floors are hardwood with a long mirror on one of the walls. It's all very clean and organized: I have an appointment book. I work three nights a week, four clients a night. Forty-five minutes of anything the client wants: waltz, rumba, tango, mambo, jitterbug, fox-trot, electric slide, even just a simple slow dance.

To taxi dance, you need a theme, a really good shtick. Something to bring in the overweight, the lonely, the middle-aged, the perverted, the bearded, the balding, the clammy handed, the ex-cons, the manic-depressives, the closet homosexuals, the smelly Eurotrash visiting the States on big banking business, the occasional six-foot-tall 40-year-old dyke.

My shtick is Jackie O', circa 1963. But she wasn't the O' then, she was just Jackie Kennedy. I took it from Rhonda, a girl who was quitting the lounge. She was getting married and moving to Colorado and she said I could have her theme. I wear a lilac suit, bone-colored square-toed pumps, a cream pillbox hat, ivory stockings, bordello-red lipstick, and a black chin-length wig. And when I dance I am the quintessential hostess. I smile. I am charming. I am the First Lady.

And because Bob is a client and because I dance with him and because there is *more* that I do for Bob—I write an erotic story once a week for him—I'm touring Europe for three months on his pocket. He gave me an American Express card with a $5,000 limit and cash-advance option, one round-trip Swiss Air ticket from Los Angeles to Zurich, a Eurorailpass with three months of unlimited train travel and an AT&T phone card because I agreed to call him while I'm away. Just one phone call a week. That's all. Just five minutes once a week. To let him know I'm in one piece. And, finally, I agreed to take three days during my trip and spend it with him in

Naxos, an island in the middle of the Cyclades, off the coast of Greece. A perfect stopping place for travelers who are making their way by boat to Santorini or Ios or Amorgós.

My friend Ava is a dancer with me at the lounge, a poet, and in the same graduate program as me, which is how I stumbled upon taxi dancing in the first place. Ava thinks I'm a shithead for letting Bob fund my summer in Europe. *You may not be fucking him,* she tells me, *but he's certainly getting fucked.*

Ava calls Bob my sugar daddy. I like to think of him as my patron. There's a difference. People screw a sugar daddy. But with patrons, you give, but you don't give out. I think Ava is just jealous. I think she'd like a patron. Poets need patrons more than almost any other kind of writer. This is a statistical fact, I'm sure of it.

Athens, Greece
I'm staying at the Hotel Eolou in the Plaka district. *Hotel* is a strong word for this place. I'm on the fourth floor in a room with one window, no fan, and one bathroom at the end of the hall that is moldy and smells like feet. Athens is the most polluted city I've ever been in. Three hours after landing here I blew my nose and my snot was black. Black. I've seen a lot of different color snot, but never black.

I just spent three weeks in Warsaw for a poetry workshop. Bob and I planned for our three days together in Naxos to come right after I finish up my workshop in Warsaw. After Naxos, I've got two more months of travel. I'm heading west, to Rome, Paris, London, Edinburgh, probably even Dublin. I'm only in Athens for two nights. I'll take a train south to Piraeus and then a ferry from there to Naxos.

The poetry workshop in Warsaw was part of my graduate program, which I hate. Graduate school is something I got myself into when I decided I wanted to be a writer. But now I know that it doesn't take two years of overbearing and hostile writing workshops filled with pompous professors and cut-throat ass-kissing students—all for the low low price of 20 grand a year—to make you a writer. The fact is, you can just be a writer. Simple as that. Unfortunately this John-Boy-Walton realization was poorly timed: halfway through the program, when I was already more than 20,000 greenbacks in the hole with Fannie Mae or Freddie Mac or whatever the hell government agency it is that lends bad decision makers like myself entirely too much money.

As much as I hate graduate school, I really want that piece of paper. I want that MFA, that Mother Fucking Asshole degree, My Friggin' Albatross, as I like to call it. I want it bad. Now that I know I don't need it, I want it, because I'm pissed that it took me a year and 20 grand to learn that I don't need it. Maybe if I hadn't even gone to graduate school, I would have never figured out that I am whatever I tell myself I am. So I've essentially learned something, haven't I? It's just that I didn't learn what I thought I was going to learn.

My graduate program makes us hop the genres. The short story cost me: I've got slowly fading scars on my legs from neurotic excoriasis, a condition in which anxiety caused me to scratch my calves until they bled. I drank myself through the novella workshop and barely completed one. Poetry blows. It is too economical and requires a nauseating level of perceived depth and affected feeling. So when I found out I could do a three-week workshop in Warsaw to knock out a semester's worth of a poetry requirement, I signed up.

I figured if I was going to spend three weeks in Warsaw, then I might as well see some more of Europe, which is how the whole Bob-paying-for-three-weeks-in-Warsaw turned into Bob-paying-for-three-months-on-the-Grand-Tour. Three months in Europe for free. Well, basically for free. I had to write an extra story a week for him for the three months before the trip. A small price to pay. Because now I get to see Europe and, just as important, Trevor doesn't get to see me. This space he wanted he now has. And I hope it's a bigger space than he imagined. We can both think about what we want, but he doesn't get a damn thing from me while I'm an ocean's length away. Trevor won't get a postcard. Not a phone call.

If Bob wasn't funding this three-month space in Europe, I'd have an entire semester of poetry with the fucking hippies, and I'd be sharing a bathroom with the guy I'm trying to give space to; decisions are hard to make when you have to share a bathroom.

Bob is an environmental engineer. He cleans up messes. He goes to the problems: to Superfund sites in Western Pennsylvania, to ambiguous chemical spills outside Moscow, to newly named Eastern Bloc countries in the middle of civil wars. He called me from the lobby of a hotel in Yerevan, Armenia, this winter. He sounded tired and cold. I could faintly make out the sound of his teeth chattering. Not only was Armenia having an environmental crisis, but they were also in the middle of a heating situation: There was none.

> I miss you, he told me over the crackly phone connection.

> Screw you, Bob. I told you that you're not allowed to miss me.

> But I do.

> Well, then go buy a puppy if you want someone to miss you back.

> And I'm cold.

> Well, then go buy a puppy and a sweater.

For the most part, Bob doesn't get needy. But sometimes he can't help himself. He pushes. He wants things he can't have, and then he's forced to settle for what he gets. And Trevor gets annoyed by Bob getting needy or calling the apartment just to talk, or by the erotica that I'll stay up late writing. But Trevor doesn't get annoyed enough to make me think he really even gives a shit whether or not I do fuck Bob, which just then annoys me. And so I get mean and harsh to Bob because Trevor doesn't get annoyed enough.

Trevor loves me, he just doesn't know whether or not he wants to be with me. Trevor doesn't know what he needs. I already know that I need Trevor, out of habit, out of love, out of not having anyone else to pick me up at the airport. Which I'm hoping Trevor will remember to do. Three months is a long time to remember the date and time that my flight comes into LAX.

I'm convinced that the stories I write for Bob are helping me become a writer. Erotica requires a shitload of descriptive language—the size of a guy's dick, its consistency, the way it throbs, it's personality even; and a woman's breasts—you've got to cover the buoyancy, the degree of lift, the color of the nipple, the tone of the skin. Details. Very few spoken words. The characters rarely talk about what it feels like to get screwed. Instead it's a lot of description of body parts sliding around and in and out, and a lot of grunting and *Oh, baby*'s. It's not like other genres, like screenwriting, where what you say is everything.

I read the stories to Bob in the room where we dance. I stand in front of the long mirror while he sits behind me in a chair doing whatever it is he is doing, rubbing himself, jacking off, whatever. I can see him in the mirror, but only if I try. I focus on the words and I let my peripheral vision blur out, like when you're at a crowded party talking to someone and you're really interested in the joke they are telling or the shape of their lips or the piece of spinach wedged between two teeth and although you can see the people in the room around you, you can't focus them. They become blurry. So when I read to Bob, I can see the words. I can see me, but Bob, he's just blurry.

⟋⟍

Bob likes anniversaries. He likes to celebrate the passage of time. He keeps track of these things. Like my birthday—August

15, 1975—which was also the first day of Woodstock in 1969 and, in 1945, it was celebrated as Victory over Japan day, marking the end of World War II. This winter, Bob and I celebrated January 10, a one-year anniversary of us knowing each other. A date marking not only the beginning of our union but, according to Bob, the day in 1861 that Florida seceded from the States, just before the Civil War began. To mark the occasion he took me out for dinner, to a restaurant of my choice. He chose me, he says, so I get to choose where we eat.

Burger King.

Come on, be serious, he said.

I am serious. I want a double Whopper, no onions or mayo, a large fry, and a black-and-white milkshake.

Melanie.

Bob likes to say my name. Depending on context, tone, and inflection, just saying my name says a lot.

What? If you didn't want me to choose, you shouldn't have told me I could.

So he takes me to Burger King. Any attempts to make something of this obscure date in time when Florida left and Bob walked in would not happen. Not in Burger King. It would be thwarted by the smell of the flame broiler, the sound of people's sneakers squeaking on the just-mopped floor, the lighting. We are reduced to our most manual and basic in fast-food lines. All meaning and underlying principles disappear when a family with four kids is behind you fighting over who is going to get to sit next to dad and an old lady in a stained house dress is in front of you ordering a fish sandwich with extra tartar sauce. The importance of anniversaries is blinded by the fast-food restaurant lighting above you. It's so bright in the line, you can hardly see.

Bob chose to dance with me, to become my client and eventually my patron, specifically because of my Jackie O' shtick. There's four of us working upstairs at the lounge. Downstairs, at the lounge's bar, is where the dancers strip and strut around in pasties and thong underwear. They'll give you lap dances and rub their crotches close to your face. Upstairs is where the taxi dancers are. I'm in Room 4 impersonating the First Lady of Camelot. Ava is above me in Room 8 doing a Carmen Miranda theme. Ava is tall, dark, and leggy, adept at all modern dances while balancing fruit on her head. I'm always telling her to bag the fresh fruit and invest in some plastic replicas. But poets, if nothing else, are purists, so she sticks with the fresh fruit. Nicole is in Room 6 dressed like Judy Garland a la Dorothy in *The Wizard of Oz:* blue gingham dress with ruby slippers, to boot. Chinese men love Nicole's Dorothy. Clare is in Room 1 playing Mama Cass from the Mamas and the Papas. She's a big girl; she has girth. Clare wears long gauzy dresses, has straight blond hair, and dances light on her feet. Short, sinewy, skinny men like to get lost in her flesh, fold into her folds, press into her sagging bosom. They pull themselves into her and across the dance floor.

You'd think that people come to taxi dance for more than just dancing. You'd think they're also expecting you to get down on your knees on the hardwood floors and blow them when you've finished your tango or waltz. But I don't do that. My steady clients, and I have quite a few of them, know they will get nothing more than dancing and conversation. What Ava and Nicole and Clare do is their business. But aside from my deal with Bob, I just dance. I was surprised myself by the fact that many of my clients aren't looking for much else. These guys want to move and shake. They want to put their arms around a pretty girl who will press softly against them and talk quietly to them. These people want to be held.

Bob came to me—Bob chose me—because he remembers the day JFK was shot. The day is seared onto his neurons. Well, his and the rest of the free world who was born before 1959. His emotion-sustaining memory of this event is trite: Everyone talks about this day. Everyone has watched the scratchy eight-millimeter Zapruder film. Everyone knows of grassy knolls and the single-bullet theory and the Warren Commission Report and the Texas School Book Depository and conspiracy theories and Mafia involvement. JFK is done. We know that story, don't we?

But Bob's story is his own. JFK just happened to be assassinated on the same day. Bob was eight years old. He lived in Ridley Park, Pennsylvania, and was on the playground of Caley Road Elementary school doing penny drops off the monkey bars. Penny drops—he starts to explain what they are, but I cut him off because I know all about them—are when you hang from your knees on the monkey bar, which is about four feet high, and you swing until your head and torso are parallel to the ground. You keep swinging until you work up enough nerve and then you release, flipping your body up so that you land on your feet. If you overswing, your feet will come out too far in front of you and you'll fall backward on your ass. If you underswing, your face will hit the ground before your feet do.

Bob was swinging a penny drop, getting ready to release, working up the nerve. He was a fat kid, so he would swing for a while to make sure his thundering body was aligned with the ground. Just as he got ready to release, just when his whole flabby body was rippling upward and parallel to the ground, he heard it, in the background, where the sun and dust and crab-grass lined his peripheral vision. He heard Mikey Bustard say it, his voice cracking. He heard Mikey Bustard say that the President was dead.

And so Bob's overswing stopped. He stopped his swing but he still released and so he underswung and when he came down he fell on his face. Slammed into the hard and dusty ground. His front tooth broke in half, jutting through his lower lip. Blood spurted and spread across his yellow button-down shirt. He was sent home by the school nurse, and he walked through the front door of his house and there was his mother, already sobbing. Sitting at the living room couch, in front of the television as the newscasters showed the outside of the Dallas hospital where JFK was. Bob's mom sees her son, in his blood-stained shirt, his swollen mouth, and his puffy eyes, and she goes down.

His mom passes out. Out. Bob tells me this—all of this— while pressed against me in a slow dance to Billie Holiday singing "Love Me or Leave Me." His mom hadn't fainted. It hadn't been the sight of him, the swollen lips, the dead President. Instead, a delicately positioned sac in her intracranial arteries—a berry aneurysm—had exploded. And he would later hear his father sobbing. Bob had never seen his father shed a tear, let alone take on the physical heaving involved in sobbing, an act that scared him more than his mother's death.

The chain of events of that day from underswung penny drops to eating dirt, broken teeth, blood-stained shirts, crying fathers, and dead mothers propelled him forward. Like a bursting vein, Bob sprung. He danced with me, because I am Jackie O', because I know about penny drops, because I won't go down.

The first time Bob came to the lounge, he was a silly-putty mess of sweat and nerves. He looked at me tentatively, and then just stared at the Jackie me. I was smoking a cigarette, which is something I don't imagine Jackie doing or at least it was something I imagined that if she did do, she did in privacy, maybe as she sat on the back porch of the pink house she lived in on the private Greek island that her second husband, Aristotle, owned.

Bob stepped in the room, looking ready to scurry, like a cockroach in the kitchen with a light about to be turned on. I was wearing a summer outfit. Something Jackie would wear in Hyannisport, maybe on Memorial Weekend, when the heaviness of impending summer peeks into the day, ready to announce itself in burdensome heat. Camel-color linen cigarette pants, a sky-blue short-sleeved button-up blouse with darted breast and a flat bottom, tortoise-shell sunglasses.

This is Room 4. Isn't it?, he asked.

That's what it says on the door.

Uhm, yeah.

Name your dance.

Well, what dance do you think Jackie would have liked?

Listen, I said, removing the sunglasses, I'm not going to talk dirty with you if that's where this is leading. We dance. We dance first. We'll talk later and we'll only talk about what I want to talk about. Got it?

Yeah.

Okay, I said.

The Waltz, he said softly, I want to waltz.

Did you ever waltz with an overweight man who sweats profusely and lost his mother at the tender age of eight to an aneurysm? Let me tell you, he'll waltz different than your average Joe. He'll waltz different than your grandfather, different than your boyfriend that you've been going out with for five years and you know the end is near but you still go to his sister's wedding, different than the deep-voiced CEO you got coerced into dancing with at the office Christmas party because you got some goddamn employee-of-the-month award instead of a promotion. All of these people waltz differently than Bob. They slide and glide across the floor. They hold on, without letting you feel them holding on.

I agreed to have dinner with Bob on November 22 this year, to mark his mother's death, and although Bob was completely unaware, the date was also marking the death of my virginity. November 22 is also the anniversary of me and Trevor's first fuck. You don't forget something like that. Trevor was my first. I was 18, old for my crowd, and we had sex on his cramped and mushy twin bed in his dark faux-wood-paneled room while his mom was at the Acme buying a week's worth of groceries. I doubt Trevor would remember something like that. Trevor has trouble remembering my middle name. I like to test him on this fact sometimes. Despite our having lived together and known each other for seven years, he consistently answers this question wrong. My middle name is Harper, which is my mother's maiden name. But he's guessed everything from Rebecca to Sophia to Farrell (that was a close one, though). Harper.

We go to Bob's mother's grave, and he puts yellow and red tulips down. Then Bob takes me to a Thai restaurant. I love the way Thai people are so small and docile and swift. They move by you like a wispy breeze, there and then suddenly gone. Bob was in a good mood, even though the anniversaries of deaths aren't festive occasions, at least in my book. He was chain smoking and waving his hands about as he talked. Bob had brought a bottle of wine because the Thai place didn't have a liquor license.

I love BYOB, Bob said to me. All the tension of the waiters trying to beef up their tip by selling an expensive wine is gone. The waiters are probably the sons and daughters of the owner. They don't seem to care that much about their own personal gains— the tip. Their loyalty is driven by something altogether different than the almighty dollar. At least it appears that way.

My preference for the BYOB is much less philosophical, I said to Bob. I simply like the abbreviation. Bring Your Own Bottle, Bring Your Own Babe, Bring Your Own Bullshit, Bring Your Own Baggage.

Bob laughed at me.

That's a good one, he said, Bring Your Own Baggage. I like that.

Well, that's what it is—what this is—isn't it? Celebrating anniversaries of people dying strikes me as a Bring Your Own Baggage kind of meal, wouldn't you say?

No, not necessarily, he said to me. Maybe we have a little less baggage in our lives when we mark the death. Maybe acknowledging these things keeps us from getting the baggage.

I think you're in denial, Bob.

You think? he asked.

Yes, I think. You see, you come to me. Think about it. I'm the American Tourister of baggage in your life, packed and ready. I'm the suitcase, the garment bag, even the goddamn makeup case.

Melanie, why do you have to be so dramatic?

I was starting something, not quite a fight, but I was elevating the atmosphere. Because I needed to, because Bob needed to be reminded not to be too comfortable with what the two of us seemed to be when sitting nicely in a quiet Thai restaurant. He needed to be reminded of what we really were.

A toast, I said, convinced it was time to change tone and attitude and subjects.

We both lifted our glasses.

To the dead.

To the dead, Bob quietly repeated.

Naxos, Greece, June 20
Bob is here. I sense him before I even see him. Once you really get to know someone, a detection system turns on. The person's presence makes itself known in a peripheral way, like a ringing in your ears, or static. I'm meeting him in the lobby of the Hotel Venus at 9:30 PM. This was the plan we set up before I left the country. I've already checked in. We have separate rooms, of course.

This afternoon I went to the beach. I floated by myself in the Aegean Sea, half-reclined, looking through the clear-as-glass water at my toes, dangling, fluttering. When you float in this water, you see everything that is under and around you. The fear you get in the ocean in the States—of sharks, jelly fish, someone underwater getting ready to grab your ankle and pull you under—are gone. You have clarity in this sea, a stark brightness of environment, like the first few days after quitting smoking cigarettes: Invisible things appear to you.

I go meet Bob at 9:30. I wear a long black cotton skirt, a spaghetti-strap spandex shirt without a bra. My tits are small—bee stings, Trevor calls them—and I've got on leather sandals that I bought right after I got off the ferry for 1,200 drachmas. That's about four American dollars. For leather sandals. It's a steal, a total steal. Bob is sitting in the lobby, just as I imagined him—clean and showered, smoking a cigarette. I walk up to him, and something is different. He sees me, rises, and comes to me, his arms outstretched for a hug.

Bob got some. He got laid. I can see it. I can tell. You can read it in a person's body, in the shape of their face, the turn of their smile—their ears even, which will sometimes seem a bit higher on their head. It's as if sex not only pushes your senses, but your sense organs, up to new levels.

Look at you, he says, grinning.

He takes my cheek in his hand, delicately, turning my face to the left and the right, like a slow motion *No* on my part.

You got a little too much sun on your face, he says.

So who is she? I ask immediately.

Who's who?

The lucky girl.

What are you talking about?

Don't play dumb with me. Tell me who she is.

I'm smiling now, too. Games are pointless, I know, but I still like to win.

I don't know what you mean, Bob says to me.

You got laid. I can tell.

Bob looks down. He looks back up, and he stares me straight in the eyes and doesn't say a word. He reaches over to push the spaghetti-thin strap of my shirt up to my shoulder, from where it had slipped.

Melanie, really.

What? Come on, just tell me.

It's nothing, really.

Come on. It's not nothing. Getting some is something. Who are you kidding?

We go down the street to a small outdoor bar by the water. I stare at Bob and let things be quiet. I don't need to speak. I'm waiting for his story. I light a cigarette and smoke slowly because I have all the time in the world. Bob and I drink Mythos, a Greek beer, and I talk small stuff: what I thought of Warsaw and the poetry workshop; the flight to Athens and how everyone on the plane clapped after the plane landed, a courteous and common gesture; how you couldn't flush your toilet paper in my hotel in Athens but instead had to throw everything out in a small and grimy trash can.

I tell him everything that is obvious: how Athens is dirty and chaotic, how I got in a loud and heated fight with a taxi driver who tried to charge me 50 U.S. dollars for an eight-minute ride from the airport to the Plaka, how I saw two dogs who were fucking that got stuck in the coital pose, how I can't wait to go see Rome and the Sistine Chapel. But my flat and monotonous tone is annoying him, because I am not giving up, because I won't give him any more until he tells me about getting laid. The cards are on the table. Bob is flush.

> Her name is Diane, he finally says. She's a temp in our office. She came to a happy hour we had a few weeks ago, and we talked a lot that night.

Bob starts to talk more quickly and without reluctance, like he is freed.

> And it surprised me. She surprised me. She's from Philadelphia, too. Isn't that funny? We practically grew up in the same neighborhood. Different high

schools of course, but still. What are the chances? And then the next night we went out for a movie. I asked her to the movies, and she said Yes and we went.

And?

And well, there's not much more to say. We've seen each other about six or seven times since you left.

Bob got laid.

It's not like that, and don't talk to me in the third person.

So, are you going to marry this girl? I ask him, teasing him.

How should I know?

Well, I assume you're going to go out with her again, correct?

She's picking me up at the airport.

She's picking you up at the airport? Holy shit, Bob, this is serious. The airport retrieval means you are in a relationship. It's like practically being engaged.

Not quite, he says.

Well, did you tell her about the person you were
meeting up with in Naxos?

Now you're talking about yourself in the third person, Bob says, ignoring my question and trying to
make a joke.

I didn't think so, I say, answering my own question
for Bob. Well, I don't know about you Bob, but I
need another drink.

Bob turns around, away from me, and tries to get the bar-
tender's attention.

After drinks, we went to Koutouki Taverna, a tiny place,
like all restaurants on the island, where you sit at rickety
wooden tables on the street and skinny cats meander between
chairs, looking up and mewing. There was a cool night breeze
blowing and the buzz of exposed light bulbs on wires strung
above dimly burned a glow. An old man sat us. He was short
with age, tanned and creased by a life on an island. Without a
word he disappeared for a moment and then reappeared, carrying two tall glasses of ouzo mixed with water, a warm and
cloudy drink that you are instructed to sip slowly.

Sip, sip. Don't drink fast, he tells us as his knobby-
knuckled hands put the glasses in front of us.

Then a heavy-set old woman, probably the old man's wife,
appeared at the table carrying a huge tray that she rested on the
table. On the tray are about ten little aluminum trays of different

foods. You pick what you want and get charged per tray. She tells us this in broken English, but we quickly get the picture. We take a tray of fava, kalamari and eggplant, tomato and cucumber salad, tzatziki, and stuffed grape leaves. You get to choose what you want, but all of the big choices are already made for you.

June 21

I sipped too much ouzo last night, and so I slept late today. And all I wanted to do was shop, which, anywhere in Greece, is inexpensive. But before I met up with Bob for a late breakfast, I walked down the street and found a bank machine, tucked in the back of the small travel office where I booked my ferry back to Piraeus. I withdrew as much drachma as I could— 240,000—which is about 800 U.S. dollars. I needed to know that I'd have it—there, with me. I knew the exchange rate was going to suck when I went to Rome, my next destination, but I didn't care. I needed to know that I had that money because I knew now that Bob had Diane, and it all begins to become clear to me that what I need and what he needs is changing, daily. The exchange rate was going up; I could feel it.

Bob and I shopped for hours. I got a leather journal, a light-brown leather backpack, a silver and lapiz ring, a set of worry beads that the lady in the shop told me you are supposed to give to a man so he can swing them with his hand when he worried about something, an ornament—a glass blue eye—which is supposed to ward off evil and bad will, a white cotton sweater, a handspun blanket with a Greek sign-of-life pattern. Bob kept paying, so I kept shopping. He offered to take the purchases home with him, so I didn't have to drag them with me for the next two months or pay the high shipping costs, not to mention customs.

Well thanks, I said.

No problem. Happy to carry some of your baggage, he said, grinning.

Ha ha, I said with an intentionally affected laugh. If tchotchkes are my baggage, Bob, then I'm not doing too bad, emotionally speaking, am I?

No, not too bad, Bob said, but don't forget, tchotchkes are cheap.

Later that afternoon, after shopping, Bob went to take a nap and I sat on one of the decks of the Hotel Venus. The view is clear and white: rooftops of homes and churches, and in the distance, overlooking the Aegean, is Portara, an entrance to an unfinished temple. Portara stands there, like a lower-case, geometric-shaped *n*, white and alone and staring out at the sea.

Kiki, the woman who owns Hotel Venus, ten small but meticulously clean rooms, was bringing up fresh towels. Kiki passes me, saying *Hello Hello* with her thick Greek accent, and scurries back down the steps. I could hear the sound of children fighting with their mother at the house next door to the hotel. I was sitting in the sun without sunblock reading *Hello* magazine, a British tabloid that is thick with colorful pictures of British celebrities and royalty. It's the British version of *People,* and about the only magazine on this island in English. I'm reading about Robbie Williams, former lead singer of Take That, who just got engaged to one of the singers of All Saints, an all-girl band comprised of perfectly breasted, flat-bellied girls with thick accents and a mass following.

Kiki comes back up the stairs and she is carrying a white, netted bundle. She opens it and inside is a handful of Jordan almonds.

> Take some, she said to me. Yes, take. You get husband then.

> Husband? No, no, he's not my husband. He's just my friend. Only a friend, I said, attempting to correct her. Getting ready to try to explain the dynamics of me and Bob to this woman.

> No, no, she said, eat these and it bring you husband. Next time you come to Hotel Venus, you bring the husband you will meet now that you eat almonds.

> An almond will bring me a husband?

> Yes, she said nodding her head up and down quickly, gray strands sprouting from a mass of black hair.

I took one and placed it in my lap. But Kiki took my hand and put it back in the full white-netted bag, urging me to take more, as if she knew one Jordan almond wasn't going to get me what I need. This was too simple. An almond for a husband.

Trevor would make a lousy husband. He'd probably get stoned before the wedding and show up late, all shits and giggles with that grin of his that spreads across his softly bearded face that loses me every time. I get lost in that grin and forget about what I need. I had a patron, whose status as a patron was becoming questionable, and I had a boyfriend, who wasn't going to be my husband. But now I had the almonds, so I put them in a small plastic bag with Greek written all over it—a store bag, from one of the many tchotchkes that I had bought—and I put the bag of almonds in a small satchel that held my passport, credit card, and cash and that I wear around my neck when I'm out and about, under my shirt. It lays against my skin, right over my heart.

June 22

Bob is out swimming. I can see him from here, but I can barely see his face because I didn't put my contacts in this morning. I can't tell if he is smiling or at peace or thinking about Diane or staring at his feet. I thought I saw him waving his arm a minute ago, like he was signaling for me to come out there. But I pretended to be engrossed in slathering sunblock all over me. I'm lathered up and slick.

I'm not ready to swim yet. I'll go in later, when the afternoon sun is too much for the American and German tourists that are speckled across this beach. A pack of skinny dogs linger at the shoreline, just a few feet from my towel. They are mangy and tired looking, like they need a good meal and a soft place to rest their heads. I'll wait to swim until the tourists make their way off the beach to little stands that sell fresh gyros and frappes and Mythos for what seems like pennies. I'll wait until I've got the water to myself. I can't swim with Bob or any strangers for that matter.

Tomorrow I catch the ferry back to Piraeus, and then I'll spend one more night in Athens before I fly out to Rome. I'm ready to see the Eternal City. I want to see the ceiling of the Sistine Chapel, the two hands almost touching. I want to walk up the Spanish Steps. I want to drop my coin in Trevi Fountain. I want to see the Colosseum and the Forum—I need to go see the ruins.

CARDIFF-BY-THE-SEA

MY DAUGHTER, MIRANDA, IS SPENDING the summer with me here in Cardiff-by-the-Sea. She rented a car so she can drive down the I-5 to San Diego State University, where she is taking a ten-week intensive course on Virgil's *Aeneid*. I don't have a car because I am blind.

Miranda lives in England. She just finished her second year at Christ Church, one of Oxford's prestigious colleges. She's earning a degree in the Classics. My daughter was conceived, born, and raised by her mother, Kathleen, in Aberystwyth, Wales. Twenty-two years ago Kathleen and I made Miranda, and for 22 years Miranda's life has been an ocean away from me.

When my ex-wife, Judith, and I were still married, we'd go to Aberystwyth every winter for a week to visit Miranda. Judith and I would stay at the Sunnymede Guest House, just blocks from where Miranda lived with Kathleen. Judith would make

fun of the Welsh accent and the names of their towns: Cwm-
bran, Merthyr Tydfil, Ystradfellte, Nant Gwynant, Betws-y-
Coed.

"I'd say Vanna White needs to come in here and sell these
people a few vowels," Judith remarked.

This is the first time Miranda has stayed with me for an entire summer. She usually stays for just a week or two. I have always wanted more, but constantly disrupting my child's life for
my own desires is easier said than done. Even though I wanted
to see her and be with her more than a few times a year, she had
her life with her mother in Wales, and I had my life with Judith
here in California, and well, we've had to live our lives as they
were.

I love her presence in my home this summer, the discovery
of her routines. I love the smell of her shampoo. I love how
loudly she eats her cereal, how late she stays up at night. I love
how my dog, Buck, a fat and lazy golden retriever, has begun
following her around the house, how he will stay with her until
she goes to bed and then make his way into my room. I hear all
of this. I imagine he just sits there with her while she watches
late-night television (I purchased one just for her arrival this
summer), by her side, and knowing this makes my heart swell.

When I awake in the morning, I am hyperaware that my
daughter is here in my home, asleep, comfortable. And it is this
knowledge that makes it possible for me to leave for the day—
just knowing she is here, living the everyday with me. I have
two jobs. I teach a night class in philosophy at the local com-
munity college. And I also work three days a week at Scripps
Encinitas Hospital in the Radiology Department. I develop ra-
diographs. The job is simple, a no-brainer: There is a two-way

box outside the darkroom, and the technician drops film cassettes he or she just shot. I pick up these cassettes from inside the darkroom, load them into the processor, push a few buttons. Hospitals notoriously have trouble keeping this job filled. Most developers usually last three months tops. Spending an eight-hour day in the pitch-black darkroom messes with people's circadian rhythms: They get insomnia, they get bad headaches, they become clinically depressed. I'm in the dark 24-7, so my circadian rhythms are unaffected by the darkroom.

When I came home from work yesterday, Jordan, my next-door neighbor, was in the kitchen with Miranda. I could hear them talking; his distinct southern California surfer accent and her Welsh one were bouncing off the walls, a mixture of tongues and inflections and tones.

"Hey hey, Mark," Jordan said to me. "Brought your blender back and found this lovely lady here who claims she's your daughter." Jordan had borrowed my blender weeks ago for a margarita-themed happy hour he had hosted.

"I wasn't going to let him in the house at first," Miranda chimed in, "I thought maybe he was one of those Amway salespersons you keep warning me about, or a Hare Krishna or something."

"Yeah," Jordan said, "You know how those religious fanatics are always brandishing electronic appliances."

Jordan and Miranda start laughing at this, and I force myself to join in, even though I was immediately nervous. I didn't want Jordan chummy with my daughter. Simple as that. My daughter is beautiful; her face feels like her mother's looked. She is smart and funny and independent and strong willed with a great wide-open future. Jordan is a 27-year-old boy whom I am immensely fond of, frequently amused by, occasionally concerned about, but he wants nothing more in this world than the freedom to surf. And here they were in the kitchen having a conversation—only a light conversation—but my panic buttons were going off.

After Jordan left, Miranda announced to me that Jordan offered to teach her to surf.

"I'm not sure I'm comfortable with you learning to surf from him," I said.

"He'll treat me with kid gloves," she said. "Besides, he's your neighbor and you trust him enough to lend him appliances," she replied.

"But you're not an appliance, Miranda."

"Don't you think you're being a bit paranoid?" she asked.

"I just don't want you to get hurt."

"Get hurt?" she asked.

"Surfing can be dangerous," I replied.

"I'm an excellent swimmer—hell, I grew up by the sea. What's the worry?"

"No worry, I guess," and I dropped the subject because it was too hard to explain that my worry had absolutely nothing to do with surfing.

I met Miranda's mother in January of 1969. I was on leave, marking the end of my first tour in Vietnam and the beginning of my second. I was spending my leave with Patrick, a buddy from my troop. We were backpacking through Great Britain. A lot of guys went to Bangkok or Malaysia for R&R, but being in those places was too much like being in Vietnam: hot, airless. The only difference was that you didn't have to carry a gun or walk around all day with your heart in your throat, wondering if you were going to get yourself killed. Great Britain provided the contrast I needed before embarking on my second year of a daily routine of insurmountable chaos and fear: crisp cold weather and thousands of miles' distance from a dense jungle that was so hot and alive and loud, so ultimately suffocating and deadly.

Patrick and I stopped for a few days in Aberystwyth before heading over to Scotland. Aberystwyth was a university town swarming with undergraduate students. The town was on the coast, with a crescent-shape curve of houses lined up along the beach. I met Kathleen at the camera obscura, a small tourist attraction up the hill from the beach. The camera obscura was a giant camera positioned in a large room. Underneath the camera was a flat, circular screen, much like a movie screen but on the floor. The camera filmed, in real time, the movement and activity on the beach road, which it projected onto the circular screen. It was voyeuristic: watching the people moving across the screen, going about their lives.

People were flowing in and out of the room, looking at the people on the screen, then moving on. But I was transfixed by the camera obscura's projection of the everyday, by the beautiful girl with black hair who was standing across the room. Patrick had his fill after ten minutes and left me in the room to stare while he went to catch a small-gauge train to Pont-ar-Fynach to see the waterfalls. I finally spoke to Kathleen when we were the only ones left in the room. She told me she was from Scotland and was a student at the university. I told her I was from the United States but that my current mailing address was South Vietnam. She said she came to the camera obscura frequently, to watch the people, to watch the everyday.

Later that evening, she joined Patrick and me at a pub and drank pint after pint of Carling beer with us. And the next day she let me smell her hair and kiss her mouth, and then we made love in the room that she rented from an elderly couple, a tiny room with a window that looked out to the cold waters of the Ceredigion Bay. Wales is a wet country. Fertile. Lush. We made love for three days and nights. And almost two months later, when I was walking a path on the edge of a rice paddy field along the Tan An Delta, I met my fate with another lady, a totally different lady altogether: a Bouncing Betty, an explosive that propels itself about four feet up into the air and then detonates, sending a nightmare of ball bearings everywhere, killing the guy who stepped on the lady land mine and injuring anyone—like me—within a couple hundred meters of it. I met this lady when she killed Skip Paterson and Kyle Renshaw, and she left me blind to the rest of my world.

Three mornings a week at the crack of dawn, Jordan takes Miranda out to the beach, just two miles from the house, for her surfing lessons. Even though Jordan lives just a few houses down the block, he comes to the door each morning to get Miranda, a chivalrous act I can't help but silently commend him on. Today I could hear the music from his car radio, the tear-provoking voice of Carl Wilson from the Beach Boys singing "God Only Knows."

If you should ever leave me, well life would still go on believe me, Carl was singing.

I sense that Jordan is like some kind of dream to my 22-year-old daughter, who wants to try everything that is new, everything that is American, everything that is unfamiliar. I hear Miranda leave the house, and the sound of Carl Wilson starts up again. I hear her shout at him, a shout mixed with laughter, telling him "to turn the bloody music down before you wake the rest of the block." Then the car pulls off, not peeling out or anything. Jordan knows what precious cargo he is taking with him to the waters of Cardiff-by-the-Sea.

I am trying not to be alarmed by Miranda, by her joy, by the way her happiness pulls like an undertow with each day she surfs with Jordan. I am hoping it is some Gidget-like trance that has overcome her. I am hoping it is the thrilling fear of it all, of standing up unsteadily with nothing but a piece of fiberglass between her perfect toes and the moving ocean. I am hoping it is all of this. I am hoping it is not just Jordan. What if it is simply Jordan?

"How are the surfing lessons going?" I asked her this morning. Miranda is distracted and cursing under her breath, trying to find her car keys. I remember hearing the clinking sound of them being put on the coffee table the night before, so I tell her to check there.

"Christ, this is bad when the blind man finds the missing keys," she says, walking back into the kitchen and jingling the found keys.

"Well, how are they going?" I asked again.

"How are what going?" she said, still distracted.

My daughter is in love.

"Your surfing lessons. With Jordan."

"Oh they're grand," she said, "I can stand up for almost 30 seconds now, but it seems like forever when you are up there, you know."

Jordan comes over at night a lot now, too, so they can go hang out, grab a bite to eat. *We're just going to kick around*, she says, becoming adept at American lingo. When Jordan knocks on the door at night, Miranda's frantic rushing around the house comes to a halt. She slows her footsteps, conscious of her movement—probably to seem cool to him, not overanxious, not that in love. Miranda is too smart for gushing. She knows this. And she knows that I don't approve. It's not even so much that I don't approve—it's just that it's Jordan, it's just that she just met him, it's just that he lives in a house with about four other guys with a bathroom so dirty that I can smell it from the driveway, it's just that he didn't finish his college degree and he isn't even on his way to doing so. There are so many of these: *it's just*.

It is more than just surfing. More than just a wave. The tide has come in.

I ask Miranda too many questions when she goes out with Jordan. She handles my concern deftly with her humor. She does the same thing to Jordan, playfully putting the men in her life in their place. Last week Jordan was in the living room watching a basketball game on the television, waiting for Miranda to finish getting ready. I could hear him yelling at the television, his favorite team losing perhaps. Miranda walked into the room, smiled at him no doubt, and said, "Stop yelling at the telly, Jordan; it can't hear you."

My worry for Miranda is never ending, an aspect of fatherhood that nothing, not even the battlegrounds of Vietnam, could prepare me for. But the worry is more bearable when she is here. This extended visit is causing more worry, more bearable worry than I anticipated. And her visit this summer is more than visiting. This is the everyday. It feels like the camera obscura is pointed right at us.

After I met the Bouncing Betty and the world turned black, I was sent home to pick up the pieces of my life. I think now how hurt Kathleen must have been by the sudden end of letters from me with no explanation, and the letters she sent me being returned to her, unopened. I think how scared she must have been, too, discovering she was pregnant, trying to get in touch with me to no avail. (After all of the unopened, returned letters, she gave up. She made no phone calls to try to find me, to tell me. She assumed I wanted only what I had taken and would never want anything else.) But I did not know she was pregnant, because I did not let anyone open her letters. I had them sent back, and then they stopped coming. I was blind and young, double-blinded by my anger. By the time I stopped being so angry, years later, I decided that all of that—Kathleen and Wales and Vietnam—was the past. The beautiful foreign woman and the cold and hot foreign countries were too much to bring back once I stopped being so angry. I went on with my life. I met Judith and fell in love, and the next thing I knew I was 32 years old with a wife, a dog, a degree in philosophy, a job at Scripps. A life. I was in the middle of life, and then one day in the middle of my life I got a phone call from Kathleen telling me I had a ten-year-old daughter named Miranda, another life, mine.

From the moment Miranda came into my life, my relationship with Judith began to slowly and irrevocably crumble. For years Judith and I had been trying to have a baby, and Judith just didn't become pregnant. Then this child arrives in our life, but it was a child that was only mine. It felt like two children from then on: the ghost of a much-wanted and unborn child, and the newly discovered, unintentional Welsh girl named Miranda. These children hung over our house like a mist, touching our brows and faces and hands, making everything in our marriage limp and damp, something that eventually could not hold itself together any longer.

The phone rang that Saturday afternoon. Judith answered the phone and slowly said a lot of *Uh-huh*'s and *Yes*'s, with a tone that I would come to be familiar with over the following years, a tone of unfairness striking.

"Mark," Judith said, sounding confused, her voice cracking, "it's for you. She says her name is Kathleen."

The world rushed into our kitchen. Judith and I were there in Cardiff-by-the-Sea and suddenly Vietnam and Wales came back with frightening speed, the way things come back so much faster than you could ever leave them.

"She says she knew you during the war," Judith said, and I heard her walk toward me to give me the phone, probably with her hand over the mouthpiece. "She sounds British or Irish or something."

"Scottish," I said, involuntarily. The word just fell out of my mouth while I was taking in a deep breath.

Last week, the surfing lessons stopped suddenly. Nothing else stopped, just the lessons. Jordan coming over, him calling, Miranda running off to be with him—all of that didn't stop. There was a new silence in the morning. I thought the end of the surfing lesson was a lot of things: Miranda being too interested in the everything else of Jordan to care about surfing anymore, her preparing for her eventual departure, which was just two weeks away, her class work taking up too much of her late evenings, leaving her too tired to get up that early for surfing. But all of these excuses don't make sense. Miranda is tough and has the endurance of an ox. Lack of sleep and being in love and all of those other things wouldn't stop her from learning something new. She's the kind of girl who, once she learns something, has to master it. This is a girl who is studying Latin and Greek for Christ's sake.

Jordan still surfs every morning. Jordan will surf every morning for the rest of his life. It doesn't matter how much or little sleep he got, he'll go out and tackle those cold waves, the ice-splash of the Pacific Ocean, reminding him most of all, I suspect, that he is alive. Extreme temperatures do that. I remember the heat of South Vietnam, a heat that made my hands swell and my feet feel two sizes bigger than my boots, a heat that reminded me I was alive.

The surfing lessons have stopped, but a new routine has been added to the morning. I hear Buck, early in the morning before I get up. He wanders over to the bathroom at the end of the hall, the bathroom that Miranda uses. He sits there and listens to

Miranda in there, the door closed I'm sure, he sits there and listens to the retching sounds that I also hear. He sits there and waits.

⌇

The first time I went to see Miranda, I went alone. How to do this? To be with Kathleen, after so many years, after losing my sight, after losing my life as I knew it then. My youth was tucked neatly away in a trunk with medical records and old uniforms. To slip back into Kathleen's life, to slip into my new life—as a parent. I was so nervous, but when Kathleen picked me up at the airport, her voice immediately soothed me, reassured me, prepared me for all of this, this daughter of mine I was going to meet, her words like soft winds across my face.

"Would you like a few minutes alone before I go get her, Mark?" Kathleen asked. We had arrived at her house after the long drive from the airport, during which all uncomfortable possibilities were washed away in catching up with each other, hearing about each other's spouses and lives. I met her husband, Frank, first. He was waiting for us in the foyer, helping me in the house, taking my bags. His voice was deep and calm, and I liked him immediately for making me feel so welcome. I imagined he was as scared as I was.

"No, I don't need any time," I said, anxious and ready to get it over with, to begin.

"Okay, well, let's go to the living room. I'll get Miranda, and Frank will make us some tea."

I followed Kathleen, and took a seat on the couch. A few minutes later I heard them coming into the living room. I sensed Miranda immediately. I could smell her and know her immediately as mine, as my child. It was something I can barely articulate to this day, being overwhelmed by knowing something is yours. By possession.

"Hello, Miranda," I said immediately, through a voice of nerves and fatigue and elation.

"'Ello there," she said firmly. "Mummy said you are blind," she stated, matter-of-factly.

"Blind as a bat," I blurted out nervously, not knowing what to say.

"Oh, yes, that's very funny," she said. "Because actually bats aren't blind. It's a myth, you know. But we learned that they don't really have great eyes, not at all. So they rely on their hearing."

"*Blind as a bat* is an expression we use over in the United States," I said. I did not know what to say or do. A daughter is a precious thing. I had just received my first and only. I held it all very delicately, not wanting to drop or spill or break a single thing.

"If you're blind," Miranda said to me, "then you won't ever be able to see what I look like, will you?"

"Well, no. But I used to be able to see. So maybe one day you can let me touch your face. If I touch your face I can imagine what you look like."

"Oh, okay," she said and paused for a moment, "Well, what should I call you? What do you want me to call you?"

Miranda still calls me Mark. And although I am her father, she has not spent the everyday of her life with me. I am Mark, her dad, and Frank is Dad. As children we don't get to choose what we are familiar with; these things are chosen for us or fate makes the decisions. Her image of fatherhood had already been chosen, fated. It is only when we are adults that we get to choose, and sometimes even then we don't. I didn't choose Vietnam or meeting a Bouncing Betty. I didn't get to choose my last vision on earth: the too-bright wet green grass around the rice paddies of the Tan An Delta, the weathered and muddy back of Skip Paterson, the guy walking in front of me on the path that day. I didn't choose Miranda. I didn't choose any of this, and now here it all is, mixed together—my daughter, the darkness, all of this as familiar to me now as the sounds and smell of high tide.

Miranda is driving us to Miguel's, a Mexican restaurant. Jordan is meeting us there. Miguel's is a dive: plastic patio furniture on a wooden deck on the water, cheap prices, cold beers, and the best black-bean burritos in southern California. Miguel's is in Ocean Beach, a town that is populated by aging hippies and by college kids who achingly long for the 1960s and a time they never knew. 'Can't say I blame Miranda's generation for their longings. I worry about my daughter. I worry about Jordan. I worry about the child they made—where he or she will be born, raised, what will be familiar. I worry about their world and its diseases and hypocrisies. I worry about the evils and the darkness that they may have, because we all get our share of darkness. It comes to all of us in one form or another.

Miranda is getting ready in the bathroom, and I can hear her. Combs and brushes being set on the sink. When you are married or live with someone, there is a flow and symmetry to your everyday. The way people move through their lives, their homes, their hallways, takes on a pattern. I have come to my pattern of living here with just myself and Buck. With Miranda here this summer, my symmetry has changed. I am touched regularly now, by more than just Buck pushing his snout against me or the women I have dated in the years since Judith and I split up. Miranda kisses me on the cheek a lot, even if she is just going down the street to buy some milk. She touches my arm in the mornings when she comes into the kitchen. She gives me a hug at night when I go to bed. Our symmetry has paved a way into my heart, making that which was familiar the past, and that which is new familiar. Me, my dog, my daughter, sharing my home here in Cardiff-by-the-Sea.

Miranda told me two days ago why the surfing lessons have stopped. She already told Jordan last week. The fact that she is flying back to England in two weeks, that summer is almost over, is more complicated than any of us ever thought it would be. So many decisions. And so tonight the three of us will sit down and talk. We'll sit around a table, to have a dinner that Miranda has requested, to have a conversation Miranda wants. Miranda has so much: Oxford and her friends there, her mother in Wales, Greek and Latin to still be mastered and spoken and written. She has me, my home, and my dog, Buck. She has Jordan. She has her youth and all of these choices at her fingertips. And she has a baby in her. A baby. And tonight we will go to Miguel's and we will sit down and talk. I know nothing anymore about what I want for my daughter, for myself, for the child growing in her. All I know is that tonight we will sit down and talk.

We get to Miguel's and walk through the dining room to the deck outside where we can sit by the water, smell the salt air. I feel a gush of wind on my face, and I hear Jordan's voice, calling *Hey hey*, and it is a bit softer than usual. I know he must be coming toward us. Miranda's arm is entwined with mine, pulling us toward him. I feel Miranda, her hand involuntarily squeezing mine at the sight of this man, pulling me with her, very much with her, toward him and whatever it is that comes next, whether it is Oxford or Wales or my back porch or Jordan.

I feel Jordan step up to us, his hand touches my shoulder, her arm in mine, and they both start talking to each other quickly and softly, almost in a hush, kissing, touching, probably looking each other right in the eye, these two people who love each other and have made a baby. Their words are like waves, coming in at low tide, in a long slow sea foam of vowels and breaths.

EXPATRIATES

Last summer, when I was 15 and my sister, Linda, was 17, we went on a cross-country trip with our parents. The week after we got back from the trip, my father left the house one evening to buy a pack of cigarettes and never came home.

Weeks later, he wrote us a letter that was enclosed in an envelope postmarked "Prince Edward Island." I looked it up in our atlas—it's off the coast of Canada. My dad was not just gone but in another country altogether. The letter he wrote was 11 pages of him talking in circles, being beside the point. There was only one point: I knew he was living with the woman in the green dress, whom I saw him kissing at the Grand Canyon when we were on our cross-country trip.

And now, a year after the trip and our father leaving us for another woman and another country, Linda announced that she was not going to Berkeley in September. She told my mother and I that she was going to Switzerland with her boyfriend,

Raymond. She announced this over dinner. We have no air conditioning in our house and so in the summertime we eat dinner on the back porch. The television was on in the living room, and the newscasters spoke about Vietnam, even though the remaining combat troops had left the previous spring. Their voices echoed into the backyard and blended with the crickets and the neighbor's kid yelling and Linda telling us she was boarding a plane in one week for Zurich.

"Oh no you are not," my mother said, not shifting her focus from her dish of Hamburger Helper. "The next plane you get on will be to San Francisco, just like planned. You are going to Berkeley—you are going to college, Linda."

"I'm 18 years old and I can do whatever I want. The law says so," Linda said.

"It doesn't matter what the law says. In this house, I am the law." In the year since our father left, our mother, who had always been docile and diplomatic, had gained a spine, out of sheer necessity more than anything else.

"You can't tell me what to do," Linda replied. "Raymond and I have had it with this country. We're going to Europe. We're going to be expatriates."

"*Expatriates?*"

"Yes, Mom, expatriates."

"How much an hour does an expatriate make, Linda? Who pays for the expatriate's rent?"

"Hemingway was an expatriate," I interrupted, knowing this was no help, but unable to resist.

"That's enough, Sadie," my mother snapped at me.

"We'll figure it out. We don't need that much," Linda said to my mother.

"Linda," my mother said, taking in a deep breath, looking for air, "I'm not going to try to appeal to your rational side, because obviously you don't have one at this moment. But I will tell you something: You will not skip college, get married at 19, pop out a few kids, and wake up at 35 equipped for nothing more than a job at Woolworth's Five and Dime."

"But that's what you did, Mother," Linda said, biting and swift.

"Precisely," my mother snapped back, looking Linda directly in the eye.

South

Savannah was our first destination on our cross-country trip. We left from our home in Lafayette Hills, a suburb of Philadelphia, and jumped right onto Interstate 95. Our father wanted to knock out the Southeast right away, get the hottest part of the country over with first.

"At least in the West," our Dad said, "the air is dry. It's this humidity that'll kill you. You know that's why Southerners talk the way they do, real slow and sort of like idiots. Their brains swell from the humidity."

"Richard," my mother said with an admonishing tone.

"Dad, puh-lease, that is so rude," Linda added, raising her nose from her copy of Jack Kerouac's *On the Road*.

Our father had been billing this cross-country trip as some big adventure, some grand opportunity to see our history, to see the Motherland.

"It's the American thing to do," he said. "It's like apple pie and Fourth of July picnics and waving the flag. It's as American as lettuce, tomato, and onions."

Linda wasn't overflowing with patriotism, and the only destination that met with her approval was San Francisco, specifically, Haight-Ashbury. I wanted to go to Key West. I wanted to go to Hemingway's house and see all of the cats—Hemingway's cats. I read that Hemingway had taken a urinal from his favorite bar, Sloppy Joe's, placed the urinal on its back in his yard, and turned it into the water bowl for the cats. Hemingway's wife, Pauline, decorated it with fancy tiles and now you can't even tell that it's a urinal. I read that a lot of famous writers were mentally ill. I suspect that bringing home urinals comes with the territory.

By the time I pitched the idea for Key West and Hemingway's house, it was too late. Our plans were already firmed up, written in stone, it seemed, and we could not accommodate an extra city 12 hours south of Savannah. Otherwise, I knew our dad would have agreed to go there. Key West is a place for people who aren't necessarily walking in a straight line and, for the few months before the trip, my father's line of walking had begun to shift. He had been changing in a way that was difficult to articulate but most noticeable in the way he looked: He got stylish. My dad is a big man, six foot four, broad chested, large hands, and he looked strange in stylish clothes. He started to grow his hair even though it was too thin to grow long. He grew a beard that showed patches of gray. He wore patchouli. He bought bell-bottom pants. He bought an orange shirt. An orange shirt.

If I had known that cool June morning last summer, when the neighborhood was still quiet and me and my dad were packing up the station wagon for our cross-country trip, when my mother was obsessing over which road maps to bring (she finally settled on all four), when my sister was busy ironing her hair flat and listening to the Beatles' *White Album*, if I had known that within one year my dad would be living on Prince Edward Island with the woman in the green dress from the Grand Canyon and that my mother would be working a register at the A&P and that my sister would be announcing that she was becoming an expatriate, then I would have tried to stop it all. I would have hidden my mom's maps, burned the orange shirt, locked myself in my room. I would have been just fine not seeing the country.

～∬～

I like my sister's boyfriend, Raymond. He talks to me. He asks me how school is. He'll look through my records and make comments: *Leonard Cohen is so cool, man.* And *The Turtles? What are you doing with a Turtles album in this collection, Sadie?* Raymond is tall with long brown hair and a beard. My best friend, Patricia, says that all he needs is a pair of thong sandals and he'd be a dead ringer for Jesus.

I don't like Linda. I haven't for years. I wonder if I ever will again. But most of all, I don't like Linda and Raymond going to Switzerland.

"You know, Colorado is an option," I said to Linda the day after she announced she was going to Switzerland.

"Going to Switzerland isn't about snow," she replied. But I already knew this. I just didn't know how to ask my sister to stay.

"Raymond's mother totally supports what we are doing," Linda said. I secretly wondered if she was going to support them financially too. Not only did Raymond have no worries about a draft—the mandatory one had ended the year before—but his mother had a never ending supply of money. According to Linda, his mom took Raymond's dad to the cleaners when they got divorced.

"Mom doesn't get it. She probably never will," Linda continued.

"I don't get it either," I said.

"Christ, Sadie, I have the rest of my life for college. Mom may be worried that I'm going to turn into her, but if I stay here and go to college and do all those things that I am supposed to do, then I'll turn into her a whole lot quicker."

"I don't get why you have to leave the country to avoid all of that."

"Because it's the only way. I've really got to shake destiny up to get it off my back."

Linda was starting to lose me, and she looked like she was about to cry.

West

After Savannah we went to New Orleans.

"Hola, Hola, we're going to Nola," my father kept singing.

"What is with this Nola stuff," my mother said. "We're going to New Orleans."

"Exactly, my sweet dear wife. Nola *is* New Orleans. N-O for New Orleans and L-A for Louisiana. Nola Nola."

We stayed at a bed and breakfast on Magazine Street in the Garden District—Delilah's House. The owner, Delilah, was 49 years old with short black hair, and she had a 24-year-old Australian boyfriend named Pierce. Linda and I were awestruck at the setup, fighting to keep our mouths from hitting the floor when she introduced us to Pierce and told us how the two of them had been out the night before celebrating their birthdays.

"The actual date of our births is only three days apart," she said, with a buttery Southern drawl, "but the years between us are 25. But that's okay, cause he keeps me young," and a soft chuckle rose from deep in her throat.

My father thought she was great, "a real character," but our mother was visibly uncomfortable. *This isn't the way the guidebook described this place*, she whispered through clenched teeth as we lugged our suitcases up the staircase. My mother wanted the tourist's version of New Orleans. She wanted the picturesque houses with wrought-iron railings wrapping intricately around windows and porches. She wanted the French Quarter, with the immaculate antique stores and the big open-air French Market. She didn't opt for this.

The next morning, I sat at the kitchen table watching Delilah fry up sausages. The rest of my family was upstairs showering and getting dressed. Delilah was sipping coffee, chain-smoking, and cooking simultaneously. I was hypnotized—by her deft movements, by the expanse of the kitchen, by her walls. In every room of her house, almost every inch of wall was covered with paintings—landscapes and watercolors and scenes of city streets and ocean views and still lifes and even abstracts that looked like someone just threw a paintbrush across the room and was lucky enough to hit the canvas. I asked her where she got all the paintings.

"Some of them I've done myself. By profession, I like to call myself an art-eest," she said, with an exaggerated French accent.

"The rest of the stuff," she said, "comes from guests. My regular old regulars—the ones that keep coming back—send them to me. They like to add to the collection, sending me paintings from all over—Memphis and Bangor and Long Island and Eugene, and some from places like Umbria and Paris and Prague. Makes me feel like my home is all over the world in a way," and she sighed a heavy sigh, went back to the sausages.

"My favorite one is the painting across from the big mirror in the hallway," I said. "It sort of looks like scribble, but it's better."

"Well, I'll be. You really see things, Sadie. You have the eye."

"What eye?" I asked.

"A special eye. That's for certain. That painting is a Jackson Pollock," she said.

"Is he famous?" I asked.

"He sure is."

"Where did you get it from?" I asked.

"My second husband—and by the way, beware of the second husband, Sadie; you think you're getting a better deal than the first but usually you're not. Anyway, my second husband bought it for me in 1957, just a year after Pollock died."

"What happened to your second husband?"

"He left me."

"He left you?"

"Yes. For another."

"Who was she?" I asked. I knew instinctively I could ask her a question that, anywhere else or with anyone else, would seem inappropriate.

"Oh, he didn't leave me for a woman, sweetheart."

I paused, and for a minute I didn't understand, but then it came to me.

"Sometimes life will really throw you one hell of a pitch," she said to me, "and sometimes, Sadie, that pitch will be one doozy of a curve ball."

And just then, my father walked into the kitchen. He was wearing his orange shirt.

This is what I remember about my father leaving last year: It felt like everything for the rest of my life was going to be a surprise, a trick. I braced myself for the next popping-up puppet, the next secret chamber, the next rabbit out of the hat.

My father's sudden exit left us stranded with abandonment, with silences and storms of anger. For my sister, Linda, there were only harsh words and bitterness. For my mother, stoicism. My mother threw herself forward, going to work every day and filling her nights with cooking and cleaning and ironing and calisthenics. My mother spent 25 minutes every evening in the living room doing sit-ups and leg lifts and belly burners. She put albums on the record player and listened to Ella Fitzgerald sing "From This Moment On," lying flat on her back with her legs in the air crossing back and forth like a pair of scissors.

We all grieved separately, in the same house, among our life on a tree-lined suburban street. But it was an odd grieving. There was nothing tangible to show for this loss—no death with a funeral, no divorce papers being served and tempers flaring and plates being thrown in the heat of a bond breaking;

no visits, no phone calls, no two weeks in the summer at his place. There was dead space, gaps, an angry sister, a trembling mother. I miss my father. And I love him—I love the person who he used to be. But he vanished, so I have taken that literally. When he vanished, so did I for him, so did my feelings; they are gone, like him.

My dad left our home and our state. He left the country. My dad became an expatriate. He abandoned ship, dismantled his loyalties, hit the pike, and exited without a word. Now my sister is going to be one, too, and I don't think our family is big enough for two expatriates.

My mother stopped trying to reason with Linda; she stopped trying to talk Linda out of going to Switzerland. My mother recognized the uselessness of her words, how little they have gotten her, how the daily salutations and expressions of love can be so easily discarded. Linda was angry at my mother, for not giving in, for not approving, for not providing her with some sort of blessing, for not understanding her need to leave.

Linda invited me to go with her and Raymond and Raymond's mom, Mrs. Montero, to the airport. I told my mother that I was going to the airport. I told her quietly, as if my words were delivered softly they would hurt less.

"That's fine, Sadie," my mother replied, defeated, tired. My mother cannot win. Not ever. So she keeps her home—her homeland and her roots and her belief that these things are concrete. She can rely on the foundations of the house, the certainty that traffic will come down the street tomorrow, that mail will be delivered, that leaves will fall from the oak in the front yard, that the newspaper will be thrown haphazardly at the bottom of the driveway in the early dawn hours. I think it is what she has to cling to now. It is solid.

My mother worked a morning shift, intentionally I'm sure, on the day Linda was flying out. My mother said her good-byes the previous night, in a tense-sounding conversation with Linda in her room. I could just barely hear them through the walls. I held my breath, waiting for yelling or tears or something, but instead I could only make out the stiff replies from Linda when my mother calmly asked her to call home—collect if she needs to, when she gets to Zurich—and to check in regularly, even if it's just with a letter or postcard.

Mrs. Montero and Raymond pulled up in a gray station wagon. Usually Mrs. Montero drove a white Formula II with two blue stripes running from the back of the car, across the hood, to the front. But not on this day. I caught myself staring at her. She was stunning, with long platinum blond hair; her voice raspy and deep. But slowly I saw she was more, more than a rich woman with a big house, two horses, and a good divorce settlement, more than a bank account to roll the expatriates if they need it. I saw she is more—the way she smiles at her son— she is a mom.

Grand Canyon

"My word," my mother gushed, "would you just look at that? Can you believe it? Isn't it the most amazing thing you've ever seen?"

The Grand Canyon. Linda and I came up with a list of synonyms for it: Paul Bunyan's belly button. Guinness Book of

World Record's Largest Pothole. The pockmark of a squeezed pimple. God getting stoned and accidentally thinking he was scooping into a big carton of chocolate ice cream instead of the earth.

We were at one of those roadside turnoffs with a stunning view of the canyon. Our mother was taking pictures. Other tourists were there, too, and you had to be careful where you walked or you'd wind up being in the middle of someone else's picture.

"Richard," our mother called out, looking around for our father, turning to me and asking, "Where did your father disappear to?" She was giddy, happy; she was smiling and standing on her toes.

"I want him to get a picture of us three girls. Don't you think a picture of the three of us would be so cool?" she said, sounding strange and silly using the word *cool*.

"Haight-Ashbury is cool, Mother; the Grand Canyon is not," Linda said with exaggerated indifference, rolling her eyes at how impossibly not with-it our mother was. My mother looked wounded, but she recovered quickly.

I peered through the crowd and saw a splash of orange. My father was wearing his orange shirt. I wouldn't have been certain it was him if it wasn't for that shirt. I could just barely see him, but I could see what he was doing. He was talking to the woman with long brown hair, the woman who was staying at the same Holiday Inn as us, just a few miles from the canyon. (She was the woman my mother chatted with by the pool while I was swimming the night before, the woman my mother introduced to my father when he came over and sat next to them and said *Good evening, ladies*.) I was watching it all from the pool and I saw the look on my father's face when he met this woman. I had been going under water and trying to see how long I could hold my breath. I was winded, and I watched my parents talking to the pretty woman.

And here she was at the same crowded tourist roadside turnoff. She was wearing a bright green sundress and matching wedge shoes, with a small pink scarf tied around her neck. The crowd kept making way, parting, like pages of a book going back and forth from a breeze, so that I got to see her in full and in total but only part of my dad.

"Isn't this wonderful, girls? Isn't this such a wonderful sight?" our mother asked, forgetting about where our father was and drawn back in by the huge crater in the ground.

He's over there, I thought to myself, ready to point a finger but unable to even lift my arm.

I kept looking back, at the splash of orange, at the woman in the green dress. She was the woman I would see my father with in the parking lot later that night, at 4 AM, when I was restless and couldn't sleep and went out onto the balcony of my room. She was the woman I saw him kissing in that parking lot. She was the woman my father became an expatriate for.

"I just can't believe this," my mother said, snapping more pictures, looking at this huge gaping hole in the earth through a camera, through a tiny, narrow lens.

⌁

"They're doing the right thing," Mrs. Montero said to me. I was sitting in the front seat of her station wagon, and she was driving about 80 miles per hour down the Schuylkill Expressway. My father was out of the country, and my sister and Raymond were following suit; they were aboard a Swiss Air flight, flying above us at that very moment, on their way, gone.

Mrs. Montero was driving in the left lane, and we were passing car after car so fast that the other cars seemed to be moving in slow motion. I could hear my mother's voice in my head calling this road the *Sure-Kill Expressway*. My mother drives much more slowly on this road, white-knuckled at 55 miles per hour, her foot going on and off the accelerator so that you move back and forth in your seat and feel a little nauseous.

"Really, they are, Sadie," she continued. "They are young and they should do it now. Before they know it, they'll have a mortgage and a couple of kids, and probably not with each other. Now is the right time."

I flinched at these words, even though, in some odd way, they gave me hope. Her words made expatriatism seem temporary. Mrs. Montero drove with the air-conditioning on and the windows rolled down, simultaneously. "Best of both worlds," she told me.

"So you think they'll come back, then?" I asked her.

"Oh, of course, sweetheart. Maybe not for a year or two, but they'll be back."

"My mom doesn't seem to think that Linda is ever coming back. My mom is so mad about all of this."

"Yes, she is mad about all of this. But all of this is much bigger than just Linda going to Switzerland," she said, rolling up the windows some. She lit a cigarette and there were small wisps of hair coming down around her ear, whipping around in the wind.

"My analyst told me that when you experience a big loss—I mean a really significant loss—that every subsequent loss will resurface that first original loss," she said, shifting her focus back and forth from me to the road and back to me. "It's all Freudian."

"When I was 17 years old," she continued, "my father dropped dead from a stroke, and I swear to you, Sadie, a whole 20 years later, a whole 20 years after his death, I relived that loss. The day Mr. Montero left me, I didn't just lose my husband, but I lost my own father all over again. Once you lose, Sadie, you keep losing in a way."

Haight-Ashbury

My mother, guidebook in hand, led us through San Francisco: We saw the Painted Ladies, pastel-colored Victorian houses with immaculate flowerbeds in the front yard. We climbed Coit Tower, a monument that honored the San Francisco firefighters and built with money that Lillie Hitchcock Coit had willed to the city. Alcatraz had become part of the Golden Gate Recreation Area the year before and was open for tours. Linda refused to tour it, though. She sat and waited at Fisherman's Wharf for us while we took the ferry ride over to see it.

"Alcatraz belongs to the Native American Indians and now it's some tourist trap our government reaps the financial benefits of. Forget it. I'm not contributing to the oppression of a minority race," she said, her arms crossed in defiance.

"This land is your land, this land is my land, from California, to the New York Island," my father sang, trying to sound like Woody Guthrie and lighten the mood.

After touring Alcatraz, my father navigated our station wagon down the impossibly narrow Lombard Street—the Crookedest Street in the World. Tourists lined the sidewalks of

Lombard, watching the cars slowly bend and twist down the road, which was so swervy that from a distance, it looked like ribbon candy. I felt like a showpiece, on display, on vacation in the car with my family, with my sister and her focused demand of justice; with my father, who I saw kissing the woman in the green dress exactly four nights ago; and with my mother, sitting next to my father, reading a tour guide description of Lombard Street at the very moment we were driving down it. Reading about the way it is supposed to look. Reading aloud some travel writer's take on a tourist attraction, someone else's version of the scene, someone else's description of the story.

San Francisco is not hot or humid. In July the air snaps crisp and cool, surprising you, coming off the bay and pushing you around like you should know better than to only be wearing some little windbreaker. We drove to Haight-Ashbury after Lombard Street. We were the only station wagon slowly inching its way up and down the narrow streets. We were the only family in sight. We were a spectacle at the spectacle.

"Holy shit," Linda whispered, but not softly enough, in awe of the people and the scene.

"Linda," our mother tsked, "watch that mouth."

"What did she say?" my father asked.

"Never mind, Richard," my mother said, wanting to just let it go.

"Dad, park the car, so we can walk around," Linda said.

Hippies were everywhere, tall and short and fat and skinny, in all of their tie-dye and long hair and the way they walk on their toes, as if they are floating, the way they nod their head up and down slowly when they are speaking. They were everywhere. And so were the Mods. It was like something out of London. Guys in black straight-leg pants and leather jackets, smoking furiously and wearing dark sunglasses. Vespas were parked at almost every corner.

My mother and I hung back as Linda and my dad explored, moved forward, forgetting that my mom and I were even there as they took in the small section of such a welcoming, be-whatever-you-want-to-be city. Their pace had switched, their modes turned, gears wound. They walked ahead of my mother and I the whole time in Haight-Ashbury. It was like they were already somewhere else.

When I get home from the airport, my mom isn't there. A note is on the kitchen table: *Went to the nursery to buy some flowers.* I take the note, fold it neatly, and place it in my pocket.

I go upstairs to our bedrooms. My mother's room—what used to be my parents' room—is orderly, arranged. Her bed is made with military precision. Coins could bounce off it; dust is excluded from this place. In the corner I see five brown grocery bags, filled with my father's clothes, some shoes, a few sweaters. It is his stuff, which has not moved from the drawers or closets in the past year. My mother has recognized her loss. Our loss. The bags are packed.

I walk into Linda's room. The closet is half empty, but not much else has changed. Her bed is unmade. Her dresser countertop is sticky from spilled lotions and oils. A framed picture by the mirror: she and my father in San Francisco. They are standing there in the picture, my dad and Linda, at the intersection of Haight Street and Ashbury Street. They are at crossroads.

I hear the car pull up in the driveway. I look out Linda's bedroom window and watch as my mom gets out of the car. She looks tired, her face is puffy. I know her eyes must be red. I know she must have been crying. She opens the back door of the car, and brings pot after pot of flowers out—dahlias, zinnias—placing them on the ground in front of the porch, where later I will help her plant them.

WAXING

I'LL WAX ANYTHING. I'll wax eyebrows, armpits, bikini lines, above the lip, under the chin, across the back. I'll wax a hairy ass. I'll wax down there, around the scrotum. I'll even wax those pesky black hairs that come up around a woman's nipple. I'll take care of them.

I still do manicures and pedicures, but most people come to me for waxing. It's my specialty. Hair calls to me like a voice. It talks to me, makes me notice it, and most people just try to ignore these things, like unpleasant hair in unpleasant places. Sometimes I think that's what it all comes down to, this job of mine, getting rid of the unpleasantness.

One of my regulars, Charlotte, a professional dominatrix who comes weekly for an armpit wax, had a hair that called to me last week. She was reclined in the chair, her shirt off and her arms up over her head. I was leaning over her, slathering the hot wax across her armpits—we use a special all-natural wax that is infused with honey and tea tree oil. And I saw it there, peaking out from the lacy pink bra she was wearing, one of those demicup numbers, the kind that only cover half the breast and almost, just almost, show the nipple. I saw the short black hair staring at me while she was babbling on about how she's been getting collagen injections for the spider veins on her legs.

"Charlotte, you've got a titty hair," I blurted out. I know what I can and cannot say with my clients. And with Charlotte, I can come right out and say this.

"Oh, well would you look at that," Charlotte said, peering down at her chest. "I must have missed one."

"Jesus, Charlotte, I'll wax them for you."

"No way," she said. "It'll hurt to much. I just pluck them with tweezers. Plucking works fine."

"Not that fine. Look at that thing," I said, pointing at it, my finger grazing the top of her breast. "Let me wax them for you."

"It'll hurt too much, Peggy," she said, looking a bit scared.

"Charlotte, if I can see one hair, there must be at least five more hiding under that bra. C'mon, I won't even charge you," I said. The hair was begging me, pleading me to take care of it and its neighbors.

"Alright, just the left breast," she said, putting her trust in me, her back flattening back into the chair, her body relaxing.

I pushed her left bra cup all the way down, revealing a deep-maroon nipple with three black hairs about half an inch long on the periphery, right where the breast skin begins and the nipple ends.

"Don't put any of that wax on my nipple, Peggy," she said quickly as I moved toward her breast with my spatula.

"Now stop worrying yourself. I won't get too close," I said.

I dab just a small portion of wax onto the three small hairs above Charlotte's left nipple. And then I put the muslin strip on top of the hot wax, patting it down gently, waiting the five or six seconds before pulling the strip off quickly and with purpose. Just a little pain. Just a moment of pain. And for just a little pain we can all be smooth. First pain, then smooth, smooth and clean and neat, hairless, and clean. Smooth.

My daughter Kat and I have lunch together on Saturdays. She meets me at the salon, which is in the mall, and we walk over to the Food Court to eat. Kat is 33 years old. She's a social worker. She's a beauty—five foot seven, big brown eyes, all leg and skin and bones. She doesn't have to diet or do anything to get that way. She's got good genes—skinny genes—which she got from her father, not me. I'm built like a pear. Short. Bottom heavy.

Last week at lunch was the first time in a long time that Kat has asked me for something. I had spent the morning with a bridal party—the bride and six bridesmaids, seven manicures in all. The bride was going to Hawaii for her honeymoon, so I also waxed her from head to toe. I wish my daughter would meet a nice man she could marry. Kat and I were at the Golden Crown. It's our favorite Chinese restaurant in the mall. I was having Kung Pao chicken with fried rice, same thing I always get. Kat was having eggplant in garlic sauce with white rice, same thing she always gets. We're alike in some ways—ordering the same thing every time.

"Ma, I need to ask you a favor," Kat said, looking serious.

"Ask away," I said.

"Well, it's about a client I'm working with. Her name is Tammy Jo."

It always strikes me as odd that my daughter calls the people she works with clients, just like I do. My clients have wallets full of cash, drive BMWs and Jaguars, and have winter homes in Florida. Her clients are dirt-poor, crack-addicted, unwed mothers.

"What about her?" I asked.

"Well, I was wondering if you would give Tammy Jo a manicure."

"A what?"

"A manicure. I was wondering if you could give Tammy Jo a manicure, for free, of course. She doesn't have two nickels to rub together. It would be a favor to me."

"How many kids does she have?" I asked, unable to help myself.

"Ma, that doesn't matter. Listen, can you just do this for me?"

"How many kids does she have?"

"Ma, listen, this isn't about her kids."

"Does Tammy Jo have a job?"

"You know all of my clients are on welfare."

"Well, Kat, what does a welfare mother need a manicure for?"

"It's something she wants. And she's in really bad shape. I just wanted to do something for her."

"All of your clients are in 'bad shape.' Anyone without a job and a couple of kids on welfare usually isn't in very good shape, and if I start giving out manicures to every welfare mom, well, I'll be busier than I already am," I said, not trying to be mean, just speaking the truth. My opinions may be unpopular with my daughter, but my opinions are mine, and I stick to them.

"No, Ma, this woman is in really bad shape. She has AIDS. And hepatitis C. She's got it all. She's a mess. She's always saying how nice my nails look and so I thought it would be a nice thing to have her get a manicure is all."

"I don't know, I mean—"

"Ma," Kat said cutting me off, "look, she doesn't have to come into the salon. We could go over to her place to do it."

"Well, I don't know, Kat. I mean, I wouldn't know how to deal with your clients. They're not like mine, and I wouldn't know what to say to her. And I always know what to say to my clients."

"You don't have to say much of anything. I'll be there with you."

"Well," I said, pausing, "if it's that important to you."

"It's that important to me, Ma."

"Fine then. I'll do it. But this is for you, you know," and I brought my attention back to my Kung Pao chicken.

"Do you have tomorrow free?" Kat asked.

"I can be free."

"Great. We can go to her house then. I was hoping you'd say yes, so I already cleared it with her. How about I pick you up at noon?"

"Why don't you come over in the morning, and then you can go to Mass with me?"

"I haven't been to Mass in years," she said.

"All the more reason."

"Ma," she said, shaking her head a bit, all of a sudden looking like she did so long ago, like that skinny tall kid standing in the kitchen drinking a soda and telling me about her day in school.

"Hey, it's important to me," I said, giving her her own line back, but with a bit of a smile.

"Yeah, sure," she said and smiled at me, her beautiful smile. My beautiful daughter.

"I gotta go, Ma," she said, looking at her watch, "I've got a lot to take care of before I go out tonight."

"Where you going?" I asked.

"I've got a date," she said, rolling her eyes as if she was writing the guy off already.

But I smiled inside anyway. Happy to hear my daughter has a date. She's got something, something. I don't know what sometimes, but something.

Kat came over the next morning. She brought me a candle with a brass plate to sit it on, probably trying to butter me up or something. *Home Sweet Home* was the name of the scent.

I asked her how her date went and she shrugged at me. She shrugs a lot. I don't know where she gets it from, but she's got it practically down to a science. I just want her to meet a nice guy, and she only seems to meet losers. And then she spends the rest of her free nights volunteering at a bird rescue sanctuary. She's got a thing for birds. She's got a bird named Niko, some sort of tropical colorful bird, which she treats like it's a dog. She gives it baths and everything. I don't get it. But at least it's not a bunch of cats. At least she's not becoming like some crazy old cat lady holed up inside with too many cats and the smell of litter. No, not my daughter, she's got her birds and her welfare moms.

After Mass we came back to my apartment for lunch before going over to Tammy Jo's. I lit the candle Kat had given me. It smelled like autumn leaves burning, with a hint of cinnamon.

Kat made us tuna melts—English muffins with tuna, tomato, and cheese, open faced and broiled in the oven. I love them, even though now I don't have to eat them; I choose to eat them. There's a difference. Kat and I lived on tuna melts for the first two years after her father left us. Tuna melts and pork roll. That's how I did it. There was only that one winter when it was really bad. It was the winter when I was still in beauty school all day and working nights waiting tables at Walsh's Bar and Grill, just to pay the rent, just to keep ourselves in a good apartment in a good neighborhood. It wasn't a house, but we were in a good neighborhood, and all of Kat's friends had houses and so it was close enough.

During that winter my mother would pick up Kat after school and then stay with her at the apartment, feed her dinner, make sure she did her homework, and then get her to bed, all of this while I was waiting tables. I don't know what I would have done without my mother that first year after Peter left. I didn't like my mother. She was always telling me what I was doing wrong, harping on the fact that I chose a boozer to marry and make a baby with, never stopping. But I needed her, and she took care of Kat when I needed her. And what's a mother to do, without a mother like that?

That was the worst winter of my life, because bad made its way over to worse. Bad can go that way—it can find worse faster than you ever thought. I was in beauty school all day, on my feet, waiting tables at night, still on my feet. I was unhappy and tired and sore and beaten down and depressed, but so help me God, I was not going on welfare. And then it just crumbled, all of it: My mother died. She just up and died. She didn't show up one afternoon to watch Kat for me, and it turned out she had never even woken up that morning. And suddenly there was nobody. Nobody. Nobody to take care of Kat when I had to go off and wait tables for hungry construction workers who drank too much and were always running a hand up my thigh, pinching my ass, asking me to do things that I never even did with my husband. It all fell apart because I couldn't leave Kat there all by herself, alone, fending for herself. The kid was barely seven years old. What was I going to do? I had nobody and having nobody is a weighted heavy feeling, even though everything around you is like a void.

So after my mother died, I did what I had to do, but only for six months. Only six months, I swear to you. I went to that tan-colored windowless office every week for 24 weeks—I counted—and picked up the check and turned red with shame.

Kat had to use lunch tickets at school that winter. On Monday mornings, Kat would go to the school cafeteria and sign her name on a special list and pick up her lunch tickets. And then the Lunch Lady, with her white uniform and hair net and pink lipstick and ugly teeth—Kat told me all this—would give her five small white cards. When lunchtime came, Kat would stand in line to get her meal—Texas Tommies, spaghetti, or turkey roll—and she'd be like the rest of the kids, talking and giggling and wrinkling her nose at the day's menu. But then when everyone got to the register to pay the Lunch Lady, Kat wouldn't have to pay anything. She'd just have to hand over the little ticket. My daughter, in school, in her good school in the good neighborhood, my daughter who was always clean and neat, standing there with all the other kids who lived in houses and had big backyards, my daughter that winter, just that winter, with her own miniature version of the dole.

I try not to think about that winter too much. And when that long winter creeps into my mind, I make the memory wax, like when I wax above my own lip. I think about that winter, and the checks, and Kat having to use lunch tickets, and it's like the hot wax above my lip has dried, and there is someone else, not me, but someone else, taking the cloth at the right end of my upper lip, and pulling the wax off, grabbing at the cloth and then ripping fast and hard right off me, a quick, hot burning sting, and then it is gone and I am smooth. I will stay smooth. My daughter will always be smooth. I'll never have to wax her. Never.

Kat and I ate our tuna melts, had some coffee, and then we got ready to go to Tammy Jo's. I began packing up my manicuring instruments—files, cuticle clippers, orange sticks, buffers, hand creams, toners, lotions, and polishes. Kat went to brush her teeth; she's obsessive about her teeth, packs her toothbrush everywhere she goes.

"What colors should I bring?" I called to Kat. I could hear the water running. She still runs the water while she's brushing. Still. I spent 17 years trying to break her of that habit. I failed, obviously.

"Bright ones, Ma. Anything bright," she replied, coming over, smelling minty, looking pretty, and starting to rummage through my dresser drawer full of polishes.

"You mean the kinds the kids are wearing? All those bubble-gum colors?" I asked.

"Yeah, I'll pick some out. Finish getting your stuff together," and Kat gently nudged me away with a smile. Kat chose *What Fun We'll Have Tonight* red and *A Brightly Lit Sky* blue and some other colors too, like *Orange Peels and Mangos* and *End of the Rainbow* gold and *A Walk Down the Aisle* white and my favorite, *Prom Dress* pink.

Kat drove us to the Winter Haven trailer park, where Tammy Jo lives. It took almost an hour to get there. We drove far south of the suburbs, into the country, where the only kinds of homes you see are those fixer-upper old houses and trailer parks. We listened to a Beach Boys CD on the ride. My daughter is a child of the sixties. I certainly wasn't participating in the flower-power movement or free love or anything like that, but somehow it rubbed off on her anyway, that whole generation, the liberal crap, the music—it rubbed right off and smoothly coated her life. We listened to *Pet Sounds*. I remember when the album came out. It was 1966. I was seven months pregnant with Kat the first time I heard Brian Wilson sing "Sloop John B." I'd dance around the kitchen when it came on the radio. Peter was working construction and I didn't let myself make much of his drinking even though there was something in me telling me louder and louder to make something of it. But I ignored that voice because I was young and married and beautifully pregnant with Kat, and Brian Wilson sang to me from the radio in the kitchen, doing his cover of the Kingston Trio's "Sloop John B," singing—and then again, Brian Wilson singing, in the here and now, with my adult daughter, on the long ride to the trailer park to meet Tammy Jo, a welfare mom with AIDS, whose nails I'll paint, Brian Wilson sings, *Well I feel so broke up, I wanna to go home.*

The trailer park was flat and dense, the homes lined up like Legos, close together one after another, with all sorts of things sitting outside of each little front lawn of dried dead grass: machinery parts, rusted lawn furniture, cars with no wheels propped up on cinder blocks.

Kat drove her car up to a cream-colored trailer. The door to the trailer was hanging on its hinges. There was a banana-yellow Pontiac Bonneville, the size of a tug boat, already up near the trailer. There was a pot of dead flowers near the barely holding-up door. Kat was calm, unfazed. This was just another client of hers, and now a client of mine. Kat got out of the car, told me to lock up. I gathered my stuff and got out of the car. I was nervous.

I looked up at the front door. A large woman, almost six feet tall I'd say, with long stringy red hair, was standing there holding the door open, a grimace on her face. She was pale, fat, freckly. She was wearing a long tee shirt, and that's it. No bra from what I could tell, no pants either. I could only imagine if she had underwear on. And I didn't really want to know.

Kat walked toward her, expecting me to follow her, and yet I couldn't move. I stood there motionless. The woman didn't look friendly, and suddenly I was thinking that maybe this wasn't Tammy Jo. Maybe this wasn't the woman whose nails

I'd be doing. I didn't want this to be her. But that voice down deep told me. It must be.

I started to feel a ringing in my ears, because this was welfare, looking me straight in the eye. I was looking at it again and I didn't know why it had to look this way. I've been waxing and giving manicures and pedicures for countless years now and I've seen them all, the dominatrixes, the rich miserable women, the anxious brides and resentful bridesmaids, the working stiffs just wanting some nice fingernails that will last them through a weekend, the flamboyant gays who want every crevice of their loins smooth as a baby's, all of them, I've seen them all and heard their stories and I've helped make them beautiful and smooth and I've always known what to say or do no matter how much I can't understand or approve of these people's lives, no matter how much I couldn't relate to their choices. But this was different. I didn't know what to do here. What could I say, to this woman holding open the unhinged door of her home to me so I could come in and give her a manicure, listen to her story, make her life smoother? I couldn't seem to get my breath.

"Tammy Jo," Kat called out, "this is my mom. You can just call her Peggy." Kat's arm was stretched out, open, pointing toward me.

Tammy Jo didn't look at me. Didn't even turn her head.

"They cut off my cable, Kat. I need my cable, Kat," Tammy Jo bellowed. "I'm here all day and I don't know what I'm gonna do without my cable. You gotta get me my cable back."

"Tammy Jo, it's the weekend, and technically speaking I'm not working right now," Kat said, addressing her calmly, but with strength to her voice, like you would address a child. "My mother and I made a special trip here so that she can give you a manicure. Tomorrow morning I can find out what happened with the cable."

"Tomorrow morning ain't good enough, Kat. I need my cable back now," she said, getting red in the face, shaking her head down every time she said my daughter's name.

Tammy Jo still hadn't even so much as glanced at me, and I just stood there, still not having moved from my spot next to the closed door of my daughter's car. I was clutching my manicure kit to my chest.

"Okay, Tammy Jo, let's just calm down," Kat said.

I watched my daughter. I watched her change, transform: giving in to Tammy Jo. This is what my daughter does. She gives in for those less fortunate, for sick birds in sanctuaries on the weekends, for men who can't love her like she can love them, for welfare moms who don't even realize that Kat and I had other things we could have been doing. I watched Kat sacrifice, like pulling off the wax real slow, hair by hair, instead of a quick pull. My daughter goes to the weak, and she gets her hairs pulled off, one by one by one by one.

"I can't calm down. I need my cable," Tammy Jo screeched, not in a mean way, just an insistent way.

There is no weakness even in the weakest and downtrodden, I decided then and there. We can all get what we want, one way or another.

"Okay, Tammy Jo, just calm down some for me, okay? For me, please? I'll call the cable company while my mom is doing your nails."

And then suddenly Tammy Jo noticed me. Then she saw me. Standing there in her tee shirt and nothing else, Tammy Jo opened the door wider and grinned at me and I thought, *Don't open that door any wider or its going to fall off.* She was getting her cable. She was getting her nails done.

"Hi, I'm Tammy Jo. Whaddya say your name was?" she asked.

"Peggy. My name is Peggy," and I trembled a bit. "It's nice to meet you, Tammy Jo."

Kat walked over to me, where I was still standing by the car, and looped her arm in mine, leading me through the front door, into Tammy Jo's home.

We sat at Tammy Jo's kitchen table, which was sticky from I don't know what—food, I hoped. The kitchen was cramped, and it smelled like a cross between cooked meat and macaroni salad that had gone bad. My daughter was on the telephone with the cable company, which, to my surprise, was open on a Sunday. I was filing Tammy Jo's nails, which were weak and brittle. It was hard to hold the file well, with the rubber gloves on.

"This isn't just a mobile home," Tammy Jo said to me, "but it's a double-wide."

"It's a very nice home, Tammy Jo," I said.

"No, it's not. It's a shithole, but it's my shithole," she said, grinning a wide grin that showed yellowing and browning teeth.

I was speechless. I'm never speechless with a client. They can tell me about anything, about their divorce or their pregnant unwed daughter or their husband who got sentenced to four years in jail for embezzlement; they can tell me just about anything and I always know what to say, or not say, or demurely nod and *Uh-huh* them, but I couldn't find any words for

Tammy Jo. I just looked over at my daughter, who was talking calmly to the cable company but who somehow was still paying attention to me, obviously concerned about me, and giving me those reassuring nods. Kat kept nodding away, slowly, the kind of nod that said it was going to be okay.

"I wanted a Habitat for Humanity home, you know? You know what I'm talking about, Peggy?" she asked, her tone demanding my attention. "You know, where they build you your very own home, and you help some, too. You have to put in hours, sweat hours they call it. Sweat hours. Building a home sure would be sweat hours, huh?"

"I can imagine," I said, taking care not to break her brittle nails, nodding my head up and down.

"So I started to fill out the paperwork, but you know I started getting annoyed, because they get all Christian and shit on you. You see you go through a church and there's a committee and you have to be approved and all. So I was going through this church, the Reformed Presbyterian place right up the street. They helped me out when I was in rehab and all. Anyway, I'm getting all this paperwork filled out and then my mom up and dies. And it was hard. Oh, Peggy, I'll tell you. It was hard."

"I can imagine," I repeated.

"And so my mom owned this mobile home, and being that my brothers all have their own mobile homes already over down in Honey Brook, well, I got it. So me and the kids, Charles and TJ—TJ's my daughter you know, stands for *Tammy Jo,* 'cause you can't have two Tammy Jo's in the same house so we just call her TJ—so anyway Charles and TJ and me get to move out of our apartment and we get this place. Then we didn't need the Habitat home and I was glad to be done with that because I wouldn't have minded the sweat hours but I didn't want any of that Christian shit."

"Uh-huh," I said, watching Tammy Jo come up for air between these long explanations of her life, where it is, how she got it here. I kept nodding my head at her, just agreeing. I had no words. They were floating with the nail dust flying off from her fingers.

"I'm sorry you have to wear those gloves," Tammy Jo said, "It's just that you don't want to get AIDS from me, not for a manicure."

"It's okay, Tammy Jo," and I relaxed a bit, at her honesty, at her everything.

"It's hard, you know. Having AIDS. I don't look so good."

"It must be hard," I repeated.

Last year at the salon they sent all of us—the hair stylists, the manicurists, even the shampoo girls—for a day-long workshop: *Better Customer Service for Your Clients.* At the workshop they said to us that if people started saying things that make you uncomfortable, and you don't know what to say but you know you need to say something, then you just nicely repeat what they said. That way they know you're listening.

"And with the kids, you know, it makes it worse," she continued, "harder. You know I love them. I mean, I really do, since the moment they were born and all. But I fucked up so bad. I know it. It's my fuck up, and this is where fucking up got me. I've been clean for seven months Peggy, and it has been hard."

I kept nodding my head, feeling sweaty above my brow, under my arms.

"TJ's best friend, Donna, used to be over here every single day, Peggy," Tammy Jo continued, "every single mother-fucking day. To watch cable. 'Cause Donna's mother drinks her checks away and their cable is shut off more than it is on and so Donna would be here every day to watch MTV. But Donna doesn't come here at all now. Won't get near TJ. All of this hardness, you know, staying clean and my kids and AIDS and TJ's best friend won't come over."

"It must be hard," I repeated.

"Fuck yeah. And now they shut off my cable. And you know, fuck it. I don't know if anybody can know how hard it is."

Tammy Jo looked defeated, and her nails were barely sturdy enough for me to file, but I kept filing them anyway. I kept trying. And my daughter was still on the phone, her head leaned into the receiver while writing stuff down, her eyes looking tired. I wondered how her date was last night. I wondered if she had a date with a good man. I wondered if she had a good time. Tammy Jo's nails were a mess, a royal mess, all of it.

"Okay, Tammy Jo, how about you look through that pink bag with all the polishes. I have lots of colors that you can choose from," I said, saying something, something new, something different, anything. I couldn't repeat how hard it was for her. I just couldn't repeat it.

Tammy Jo picked *You Are My Sunshine* yellow, a color that reminds me of a cotton sundress Kat would wear when she was a pug-nosed, scrappy 11-year-old who used to smile at everything, even in the saddest of moments.

I started with Tammy Jo's right hand. I always start manicures with the right hand. I always start with the pinky, too.

The smallest of fingers. It is my routine, and I have come to rely heavily on routine when I have a client that makes me nervous or uncomfortable.

"What did you want for Kat, for her life?" Tammy Jo asked me as I start slowly on the pinky of her right hand. I have taken off my gloves. I can't paint nails with gloves on and her cuticles aren't bleeding or anything. It seems safe, or at least I have convinced myself that I am safe. Here, with Kat, in this room, it is safe.

"Well," I said, perplexed that Tammy Jo was talking to me mother-to-mother, about my daughter, "I guess I've just always wanted her to be happy."

"Is she?" Tammy Jo asked.

"I don't know," I said, feeling heartsick with my answer. "Maybe, I mean, I'm sure sometimes she is."

"That's all that you wanted for her?"

"Well that's alot, Tammy Jo," I said, defensively. The truth was, I only knew what I didn't want for my daughter. I didn't want her to spend her whole life with sick birds and going on bad dates. I didn't want her to wake up one day as a 45-year-old social worker all alone.

"Peggy, I may make dumb choices, but I'm no dummy. I can see your face—I can read it. You don't want her spending her life with heroin addicts."

I am silenced for a moment and I focus on her nails. I am on her middle finger now. Right hand middle finger, making my way to the index finger, brush in the bottle, tap-tap the extra polish off, on to the next finger. Index finger. I am now on her index finger.

Tammy Jo was staring right at me. And it felt like she wouldn't stop until I answered.

"I wanted her to be a nurse," I said, "in a hospital or something. Maybe a maternity nurse. I wanted her to be a nurse and I wanted her to marry a doctor and have children. That's what I wanted."

All of this came out of me in a rush toward the truth. Kat could not hear me. She knew nothing of what I said, and I was ashamed and feeling guilty for voicing aloud to her client what I really wanted for her when she was just ten feet away, on the phone arguing with the cable guy, trying to help Tammy Jo.

Tammy Jo stared intently at me, and my hand was shaking a bit as I moved to the thumb, the hardest nail to paint. The thumb doesn't naturally lay flat on a table. You have to lift your hand off it, fingers flexed in the air, to get the thumb flat. I lift Tammy Jo's hand, trying to guide it in the proper position. She has never had a manicure before. This was obvious. My regular clients instinctively position their hand when I reach the thumb.

"You know what I want for my daughter?" Tammy Jo asked.

"What?" I asked.

"I want her to go to beauty school," she replied.

"Why is that?" I asked, not sure if I should be insulted or flattered.

"Because she could do that, you know. She doesn't like school much, but she could do beauty school," Tammy Jo said.

"She's still young," I said. "Maybe she'll like school more as she gets older."

"I hope so. I bug her to do her homework, but the way I see it, I don't know if I'll even be alive to see her graduate high school. I mean they've got so many drugs and all, but they don't always work. And there's my liver, which may just go to pieces. I do know this: It is ugly—here, where she lives and what she sees. So maybe she can go to beauty school, you know, and maybe she can do hair and makeup and at least make the things around her pretty."

I am now on Tammy Jo's left hand. On the pinky of her left hand.

"I'm sure she'll do fine," I said to Tammy Jo, because you have to say these things sometimes, even if you don't believe them, even if you know that Tammy Jo's kid doesn't have a shot in hell of turning out fine, you have to say it. And I had to say it, because I wanted to believe it, too. I wanted TJ to do fine, and if I said it maybe, just maybe in some way it's like laying down a bit of possibility, even if it doesn't happen. Maybe it's a possibility.

"Kat has done fine, you know," Tammy Jo said to me, looking over at my daughter. "Real fine."

I am on the index finger of Tammy Jo's left hand, headed toward the thumb, headed toward all of her nails being coated in yellow, and as I move the brush back in the bottle, getting ready to pick up Tammy Jo's hand so I can paint her thumb, she beats me to the punch. She raises her hands, flexes out her fingers that point in the direction of my daughter—a quick study she is—and positions her hand, her thumb pressed flat against the table, waiting to meet a brush of sunshine.

By the time we leave Tammy Jo's house, her cable is back on. My daughter gets things done. She doesn't mess around. Maybe I did something right with her, I thought to myself;

sometimes it just seems that way, that I did something right. Tammy Jo's hands didn't look half bad. She seemed to like them. She kept sticking her arms out, fanning them back and forth in the air. She smiled at me.

As we pulled out of the trailer park I looked in the side mirror, watching the children on bikes and the shoddy trailers becoming smaller and smaller in my vision, farther and farther away from me.

"Tammy Jo asked me to wax her upper lip," I said to Kat, who was playing with the radio dial.

"Really?" Kat said quietly, not turning her eyes from the winding country road that we were driving down. There was no yellow line in this road to mark what side you were on, so you had to take it slow, because every few feet seemed to bring a sharp curve and the worry of an oncoming car that you may hit head on.

"I didn't have any of my waxing stuff on me," I said.

"Oh," Kat said softly, and I couldn't tell what she meant by that *Oh*. It wasn't a judging *Oh* or a disappointed *Oh*. It was just an unreadable *Oh*.

"But I told her I could come back some time, maybe. I mean, maybe, if I have the time and you have the time, too. Because I can't drive out here all by myself—I won't. I'm not coming out here by myself," I said, curtly, defensively almost. I didn't want Kat to get the wrong idea, like I'm a different person, like I suddenly don't have a problem with welfare moms sitting around all day with their cable and getting free manicures and waxings.

But the truth was that Tammy Jo had herself one hell of an upper-lip hair problem that I noticed even before she pointed it out. Those hairs, the same color as her orange-top head and sprouting, screamed at me from the soft spot above her thin, pale lip. I saw the hairs, heard them call to me, long before Tammy Jo asked me about waxing. And hairs like that need help, they need removal. Someone has to do it, take away the coarse dark unwanted things.

Kat dropped me off in front of my apartment, told me that she would see me next Saturday for lunch. Like always. I walked inside my door and immediately smelled it, the *Home Sweet Home* candle Kat had given me earlier in the day. That was dumb of me, I thought, leaving a lit candle in the house. But nothing bad happened, no fires. So it was okay, and the smell in the apartment was warm. I walked over to the lit candle. The wax had melted on and on, flowing right off the brass plate and across the kitchen table, like a path, a track, a railway line of autumn smells and cinnamon and there it stuck. It would come off, if I scraped it—but I just took my finger and followed it along the trail of wax, smooth, hardened.

Farm Wife

H<small>E MARRIED ME BECAUSE</small> I <small>CAN DO</small> just about anything with an egg.

I can fry them—over medium, over well, sunny-side up. I can scramble them, poach them, Benedict them, and make them into omelets. I can make a hole-in-one: take a piece of potato bread, cut a circle out of it using the lip of a cup, throw the holed bread and the hole piece into a pan with butter, crack the egg into the hole, fry, flip, serve.

Sometimes I throw a few pieces of bologna in the pan with the eggs. Sometimes I'll make a pot of grits. I make the slow-cooking kind, the kind that take forever to be done and you are standing there over the heat of the stove, sticky and tired and rejuvenated somehow: hungry. Sometimes I'll make toast: no butter, lots of strawberry jam. But really, it's the eggs that matter. It's the eggs that sealed it.

"I'm looking for a farm wife," Joshua told me.

"Oh yeah? Really?"

"Really."

Joshua and I were seated next to each other in a noncredit night class, *Better Living through Healthier Cooking*. The local high school offered night courses on everything from Peruvian bongo lessons to past life regressions. The cooking class was run by a tall, spindly man, Martin Mitchell, who was the manager of the local Fresh Fields supermarket. Martin took his teaching duties for the ten-week course entirely too seriously, using a condescending tone and plenty of scare tactics: *If you use anything but Bertolli's olive oil for this dish, you are not just depriving your taste buds, but your arteries will be screaming "Help me, Help me."*

I hadn't noticed Joshua at first, not at all in fact until I sat next to him during week 5 of the course. We wound up whispering back and forth to each other throughout the entire class, which, that week, was largely comprised of Martin pushing the finer points of *Tom's of Maine* toothpaste. I was beginning to wonder if the class was a live advertisement for overpriced Fresh Field's toiletries crammed under the guise of healthy cooking tips.

"What does a farm wife do?" I asked Joshua.

"She cooks and cleans."

"Oh yeah?"

"Yeah."

"Well, I cook and clean."

"Wanna get married?"

It really was that simple. Joshua and I were talking about our houses—his, a farmhouse built in 1849; mine, a crooked little house built in 1852 that sat next to a rail line and was used as the train conductor's home in the early 1900s. And while we whispered in the back of the classroom, Joshua mentioned he was looking for a Farm Wife. And when it turned out that the farm part of the Farm Wife was comprised of nonfarm domestic duties, I told him how I could cook just about anything, how I could make coq au vin, baked brie, lasagna rollups, Texas hash, chicken Kiev, caramelized onions on crostini, stuffed peppers, baked Alaska, string bean casserole, scattered sushi, turkey burgers, peanut butter tandy cakes, and eggs. I told him I can do just about anything with an egg.

The next day I went to the Drug Emporium, bought gallon-size containers of Windex, Comet, Murphy's Oil Soap, Fantastik Antibacterial Kitchen Cleaner, Lysol, Pledge, and Tilex, and I cleaned my house, top to bottom, every imaginable crevice. Under the fridge, behind the couch, the nether reaches of the floor past the toilet that for 12 months a year I pretend do not exist. I scrubbed and cleansed, sprayed and disinfected. I laid the sponges on the window sill to dry, for full view.

And then I invited Joshua over. When he arrived, I came to the door, still wearing yellow rubber gloves.

It dawned on me exactly three years ago that I wanted to be a wife. And when this hit me, I could only speculate what kind of wifehood I'd wind up in: a Doctor's Wife, a Lawyer's Wife, a Bus Driver's Wife, an Underemployed Alcoholic's Wife, a Trophy Wife.

I hadn't even thought about the Farm Wife option. I didn't even know there were Farm Wives in my geographic enclave. I was living in the suburbs of Philadelphia, for Christ's sake. I thought for certain that if I didn't end up a Trophy Wife, I'd end up a Second Wife of a Man My Age, the kind who was briefly married in his early 20s.

I had spent the first 33 years of my life either completely indifferent to or absolutely not wanting to be a wife. I look back now and see the curse of reading too much, of becoming overeducated, of wanting everything everything everything around me to the point of being distracted from wanting that boundary-defying intimacy with another human being. Up until this revelation, I was content to be a perennial girlfriend, the permanent lover without the paperwork.

The desire—the need—to be a wife was all because of my sister's husband dying. He died while they were on vacation celebrating their second wedding anniversary. They were on some off-the-beaten-path getaway at a farmhouse in Blacksburg, Virginia. The gist of the getaway is that you go to the middle of nowhere for a few weeks and live in someone else's house, some rich person's extra home that they rent out. You are in the country with all of its country charms but without all the work; someone else makes sure that before you arrive the closet is full of clean towels, the plants are watered, and the grass is cut. You just plop yourself in someone else's house, a place where you cook your own meals, you make your own coffee, prattle around in the kitchen, live—and die.

This farmhouse my sister Adele and her husband Gary stayed at had a cantaloupe patch. And Gary had to go and get himself electrocuted in the cantaloupe patch.

Adele was in the kitchen of the farmhouse making chocolate-chip zucchini bread. (Adele tells me the story every year, in detail, right around the anniversary of Gary's death. This year she repeated the story while her boyfriend, Eric, a Danish-French man, was in the backyard grilling burgers. Eric, who has an apartment in Paris, will probably make Adele a Euro Wife one day.) Gary had gone for a walk around the property with Peyton, their springer spaniel. It was hot in the kitchen and Adele could smell a storm. Adele could smell chocolate-chip zucchini bread baking and a storm. She would later say that she smelled death that day in the kitchen, but when you smell death you don't admit it. You can't say it out loud.

The storm came, raging and fierce, the whole sky darkening like blood pooling. Lightning struck and crashed around her, blinking in through the kitchen windows. Adele kept making loaves of zucchini bread, paying attention to the details, peeling and shredding the zucchini, measuring the flour, the small amounts of salt and baking soda. Nothing bad could happen to someone like Gary, someone so clean and clearheaded, someone with such flawless skin, such broad shoulders and a loving heart. Nothing bad could happen to a man like Gary, who wrapped a cocoon of safety around Adele, protected her.

"He must be in the barn waiting it out," she said aloud to herself, believing every word uttered through her full, pincushion lips.

But ten minutes after the storm passed, Gary still wasn't back. And then she heard Peyton, the barking and sorrowful cries.

And there Adele found him, in the cantaloupe patch, spread-eagle on the ground, her perfect husband's body, embers of a body, smoky and burnt. Gary, gone, like a sleight of a hand just barely felt when accidentally touching a passing stranger on the street.

A dead husband—even one that isn't your own—will make any respectable bachelorette feel the pressing need of bonding, of being a wife, not for any other reason than the dank and dark taste of mortality. I didn't need or want a big fancy wedding or a shiny diamond ring or countless photos of me in a white dress. I wanted a man, a mate, a person to make me remember that I am alive because I know, I know like my sister knows, that I will be dead dead dead dead dead dead dead one day and I want to love fiercely one person. I want to love one man, and he doesn't have to be perfect and he doesn't even have to be all that intelligent. He just has to love. Me. Exclusively. Like lightening. Fiercely.

For our first wedding anniversary, I made Joshua quiche.

The traditional gift for the first-year anniversary is something paper, but Joshua got a bacon, spinach, and shitake mushroom quiche. My husband never had eggs this way—the quiche way—until he met me. And he had never had shitake mushrooms. He usually had his spinach in a bowl, picked right from his garden, washed off, and then slathered in thick and fatty ranch dressing. I took all the things he likes and made something else out of it—something old, into something new.

He loves me fiercely, without compromise. He loves me imperfectly. He can be moody, brooding, without warning or prelude. He needs to be reminded, frequently, to lock the car doors wherever we go. He doesn't do laundry—ever. He snaps at me, although rarely, usually when he is very tired or very drunk. He snores too loud and he grinds his teeth and sometimes he wants to make love when I don't (or doesn't want to make love when I do), but he is committed, wholeheartedly, until death death death death (which will come, whether in the form of a car crash or breast cancer or some quiet natural cause in the depths of my nineties, it is coming one day I know I know I know I know I know), until death he will be here, for me, his Farm Wife.

The year I decided to become a wife, I stopped sleeping with men. We reach these points, somewhere between youth and middle age, a murky gray place, where it feels like we have to change, where something has to change. And not sleeping with anyone until I slept with the man who was my husband was that something that just had to change—that decision that had to be made, striking, without fear. I had nothing left to give until I could give everything.

I didn't want to hunt a husband down. I didn't want to trick, scheme, or trap. I didn't want to follow criteria or rule out any men on set parameters in the interest of time. I felt no rush. I just felt a need. I didn't want to read books written by happily married women with nose jobs and manicured nails and face-lifts telling me how to land a man. I didn't want to attend seminars on finding perfect love. I wasn't looking for perfect love or a perfect match—just love, love from a man, a good man, to make me his wife. (And I didn't want to read any books written by women who refuse to shave their armpits telling me that I

don't need a man, that I am valuable and validated and vindi-
cated here in my solitary singleness.) Both extremes tired me
out, made me feel defeated. So I took a deep breath, comfortable with this violence of need in my soul, to be bound, to be a
Wife, and I handed it up, raised my cup and just handed it up,
to Fate, to the blue skies over my head.

At the time this need first made itself known, I was the better half of a charming and talented yet-to-be-noticed screenwriter. I loved the Screenwriter, everything about him, and I
loved him fearlessly, without an insecurity in the world of my
flaws, weaknesses, quirks, or bad habits.

"I need my career to be in the right place before we get
married. I want to know that I can support a family before I
make that commitment," the Screenwriter said.

"But you're a screenwriter," I replied, knowing it could
take forever, if ever, to sell a script. "Let's just be a family anyway. Who gives a shit if we can't afford it?"

The Screenwriter would not take a wife until his stories
were in every theatre across the country. I imagined him, a man
of 50 or so, finally getting his stories heard, and then finally getting his wife. Men age better than women, this is a digestible
truth, and so he'd land himself a Trophy Wife, then he'd pop out
a few kids in his Golden Years, his ducks all lined up in a row.

So I stopped sleeping with the Screenwriter. He blinked:
confused, dumbfounded. He finished the story for us, said *The
End* in his own startled way. I had come face to face with loving
someone whose creativity may very well be their singular
lifeblood, their sole bond, the only spouse they really wanted.

I get my creativity out by dyeing my hair a different color
every other month (I've covered everything from the darkest

browns to the platinumest blonds to colors that don't exist in nature), by making those fancy creative-memory books (I took four classes and spend hundreds of dollars a year capturing pictures and memories into acid-free time-protective books), and by writing detailed letters to my State Representatives on issues ranging from water resource management to protesting the outstanding warrant for my arrest for my failure to pay a parking ticket that I insist was unjustly issued. My creativity fluctuates on a weekly basis. My income is a constant: I am a strategic marketer for a start-up software company. My boss, Brett, the founder and CEO, is 24 years old and my ever changing hair colors are embraced as an expression of me, of being Abigail, of my Abigail-ness. According to Brett, my Abigail-ness must be worn on the sleeve if I am to truly be strategic.

Joshua and my first date—the first part of the first date—was an unequivocal disaster. That first hour felt worse than the loneliness I carried around with me, like a badge kept under a jacket, right over my heart, that nobody could see. But it was there, metal pins sticking through the soft cotton, through my skin, a reminder of my oneness, my need.

We went out for dinner, or at least we tried to. The restaurant, a small Mexican place, was packed and we were crammed into the tiny bar waiting for a table. I began to drink tequila, quickly, on an empty stomach.

It was noisy in the bar, and our conversation fell flat in bursts of silence that unnerved me, and feeling the need to fill anything empty—space, my heart, silent moments—I prattled on endlessly about nothing in particular: about how I've always wanted to go to Australia, about the new traffic patterns on Route 202 caused by the construction to widen the road, about the fact that I needed to get out of my dysfunctional habit with my video store guy, who refused to charge me late fees for my perpetually late return of movies, thereby encouraging my bad behavior.

Joshua, polite and honest, sat there nodding, kindly, without a judging eye.

He smiled without showing his teeth.

And more silence. I needed to pee. Or vomit.

"Why did you ask me out anyway?" I blurted out with a chip-on-the-shoulder tone when one silent moment hit a painful apex.

When nervous or uncomfortable, I am plagued by spewing out inappropriate questions. Nice honest men had begun to bring this out the most. Probably because, at the time, they became everything I wanted, and I am caught off guard by getting what I want.

He looked startled. Shook his head. Grinned.

"I didn't ask you out. You asked me out," he said.

"Yeah, that's right," I said. The fight-or-flight response churned, working its way into my fingers and legs, working its way to get me the hell out of there, the restaurant, the date, all of it, the loneliness.

"Let's get out of here," he said, practically laughing at me. "Let's go back to your place and see what you can do with an egg."

We went back to my place. I put four eggs in a pan, fried them over medium. I grated fresh parmesan over them, sprinkled a bit of parsley. I served them on one big blue plate, two forks.

~✐~

"I tend to think you'd take an ax and give the farmer 40 whacks after a winter wringing the necks of chickens," my friend Jane said. I had just told her about Joshua.

"There are no chickens involved," I said.

"Well, that's a relief I suppose," Jane said.

"It's a farm but he's not a farmer. He's actually a stained glass guy—he restores stained glass in old churches and universities. He just happens to have a farm."

"So the nonfarmer who lives on a farm is looking for a Farm Wife?" Jane asked, wrinkling her nose up, like she always does when she disapproves of my choices. (She nearly disowned me when I dyed my hair, quite literally, red as a fire engine; she wrote a silly little song entitled "That Damn Omphalus" when I pierced my navel; and my self-induced celibacy could not go without comment: *Now that's a way to land a man,* she said, *withhold sex.*)

"He's looking for a Farm Wife, but the farm is more like a farmhouse on five acres," I explained. "There's a barn, an empty silo, a huge vegetable garden, and a John Deere tractor. But no livestock. No cows, sheep, or chickens."

"So would you have to cut grass and chop wood as a Farm Wife?"

"Probably," I replied. "And then there's the cooking and the cleaning," I added, deadpan, just to get a rise out of her. Jane loves me, but she has an irrepressible need to make it clear that most of my choices—whether they truly are good or bad— are a mistake. And I love her so much that I tend to euphemize her behavior and explain it off as her way of being maternal.

"This guy sounds like a cretin, Abigail."

"I don't think he is. I think he's just honest."

"Well, you don't do well with honest men."

"What's that supposed to mean?"

"Well, you don't exactly have a good track record with simple, solid honest men. You wind up sabotaging everything."

I looked at her cross-eyed.

"Don't look at me like that," Jane said. "You know exactly what I am talking about. I'm just repeating what you have complained about for years. I'm just saying that if the nonfarmer guy here is an honest man—chickens or no chickens—you need to work on getting over that honest man thing."

"Thanks for *your* honesty," I said.

We sipped our drinks.

"Well, cooking and cleaning beats killing chickens, I suppose," Jane said, and she polished off her martini, picking up the toothpick from the glass, offering me the olive.

On our second date, Joshua and I went to a baseball game. We saw the Philadelphia Phillies play an exhibition game with a minor league team, the Reading Phillies, at a small brick stadium near Harrisburg.

During the second inning Joshua's hand rested softly on my left thigh. His hands were rugged, perfect, harsh and worn.

Between each inning was a campy and cheezy attempt to entertain the audience: Between innings 1 and 2, a guy in a cart drove onto the field and catapulted balled-up tee-shirts to the sections of the stadium that cheered the loudest; between innings 2 and 3, a fat man dressed up like a Viking sang to the audience while standing in a plastic boat in left field; between innings 3 and 4 a game was played at home plate called "Who Wants to Be A Steak Eater?"

Joshua and I looked at each other when "Who Wants to Be A Steak Eater?" was highlighted across the video screen next to the scoreboard. We burst out laughing, breaking what had become an eight-minute span of silence. I was timing it. I was timing it so I wouldn't sabotage it. His silence began to fill me.

"Who Wants to Be A Steak Eater?" was videocast from home plate. The contestant, a young woman with a ponytail and a Reading Phillies hat was asked a baseball trivia question. If she answered correctly, she would win a $50 gift certificate to the Outback Steak House.

"Did you ever make steak and eggs?" Joshua asked me.

"No, I've never made them," I said honestly to the honest man, "But I know I can."

"I doubt that he was serious," Heather said.

Heather and I share an office. She is a strategic marketer, too. She is 29 years old. She's been married and divorced, twice. She doesn't dye her hair, but she wears her Heather-ness on her sleeve, literally—she is covered almost head to toe in tattoos. She's an Andy Warhol freak. Tomato soup cans and shadowy images of Marilyn Monroe cover her body. She hates Philadelphia. She grew up in Pittsburgh and talks incessantly about New York, but like so many people I know who hate where they live, she will probably live in Philadelphia the rest of her life.

"There is no way he was serious," she repeated, "Get a grip."

"I think he was categorically serious," I said.

"Really, Abigail, I think you are becoming delusional. You don't just go looking for a Farm Wife. It doesn't work that way."

"Well, I'm looking for a husband. Maybe it can work that way, at least for some of us."

People dead in cantaloupe patches—charred bodies on the wet ground surrounded by heavy tan cantaloupes that are filled bright orange and seeded and juicy and plentiful—they can change your life, make you really figure out what it is you want, even if you have to lose it two years later. Looking for a husband, pointedly, voicing it, wanting it, all of it, is not a desperate act when you wake up every morning aware, frighteningly aware, just plain old aware. I am scared of not being aware. I leave myself Post-It notes to stay aware. I take Emily Dickinson, *Because I could not stop for Death / He kindly stopped for me,* and I parody it on a bright yellow Post-It note: *Because I could not stop for a Husband / He kindly stopped for me.* Post-It notes keep me aware. Another Post-It note, a line from a newspaper clipping about some artsy film, a love story, quoting the director of the film: "What the hell is so wrong with wanting someone who is going to be there for you forever?"

I tell Heather that my other sister, Agnes (she's a Godly Wife), enlisted her prayer group to help a man find me, to help me become a Wife.

"Maybe Agnes and all of her prayer warriors are getting somewhere," I said. "Maybe the Big Guy in the Sky is trying to tell me something."

"Yeah, like that you've just met a crackpot misogynist who thinks that women should be doing all the cooking and cleaning."

Heather swiveled around in her chair, back to her computer screen, her fingers typing away, making her shoulders go up and down slightly. She was wearing a tank top, and her tattoos, the permanent fixtures on her skin, her life, moved and swayed.

On our second wedding anniversary I made Joshua oeufs mayonnaise, the French version of egg salad, heavy on the mayonnaise part.

He hated it. He smiled, swallowed, tried to smile again, but I am his wife. I know he hated it.

Fate brings us to this: failed meals, forced smiles, anniversaries and whatever meaningful way we attempt to celebrate them, it brings us to the lulls and patterns of our days, to death's door in cantaloupe patches and unknown ways.

It is no fairy tale, I suppose. This fate. It brings us to boredom and tedium. It does. It brings us to the perfect trap, the man we choose, for reasons which we cannot find on a television or in a newspaper or even from our own friends and family. We are not supposed to marry people because we can make them the one dish they like, because we can clean. But we do. Our reasons, his reasons, for choosing me, his Farm Wife, for me choosing him, were happenstance, were chance. And sometimes you've got to forget the chances and take new ones, get married, hold on tight.

I am his wife, his Farm Wife. I get up every morning and I make dark strong coffee for him before he goes off to the barn, where we keep his truck, my Toyota, and the John Deere tractor (I mow the lawn, lovingly, all five acres; it is a precise and methodical and cathartic job, my eyes swelling from the pollen and the sting of fresh cut grass). Joshua, my husband, goes to the barn, goes to his orange Nissan truck, a five-speed with only enough room in the cab to seat two comfortably. He gets in his car to go to work, and I, his Farm Wife, begin my day clearing off the kitchen table, piling the plates and bowls in the sink, running the water.

We're getting a few chickens, for the farm. Later today, when I get home from work, I'll begin working with the wire for the coop. I'll start to measure the wire, cut it, manipulate it. We're only getting a few chickens, so we don't need a big coop—just a small one, more like a cage.

PLAN B

THIS IS THE TRUTH: When you are on an airplane, there is a system to those overhead rings you hear.

Sometimes the ring is like a doorbell. Sometimes it's a crisper sound, swift and sudden, like when the elevator has reached your floor. On a newer plane, like the Airbus 320, the overhead ring is a distinct sound byte—*bomp*—what you get when you turn on your computer or hit the wrong key.

One overhead ring is from a flight attendant in first class asking for assistance from a flight attendant in coach. The coach flight attendant—the lower-class citizen that he or she is—has to either pick up a special black phone in the back of the plane or mosey up to first class and find out what is needed.

Two rings occur precisely before the pilot comes on the overhead speaker to make an announcement, something perfunctory, standard: *Flight attendants please prepare the cabin for landing.* Or *Please remain in your seats while the Fasten-Seatbelt sign is lit.*

Three rings is the pilot or copilot signaling a flight attendant to come to the cockpit to attend to some small and basic
need: a cup of coffee, some tissues, a candy bar, PeptoBismol.

Four rings mean one thing: Trouble. Big trouble. Four
rings signal the flight attendants to drop everything they are
doing, then and there, but in a way that doesn't look harried or
even noticeable, and to haul ass up to the cockpit. Four overhead rings mean it's time for the cockpit and the rest of the
crew to put their heads together and figure out Plan B. Four
rings mean that Plan A—i.e., takeoff, beverage, movie, bathroom, landing—has all gone to hell in a handbasket. The hy-
draulics aren't working or two engines have failed or the pilot
received word that a bomb is on the plane. When four bells
ring, Plan A—you are going to your brother's wedding in Seat-
tle, or to Des Moines to see your niece graduate college, or to
Dallas to meet up with the guy you are sleeping with (not in
love with, but sleeping with despite the travel required because
there is no one local to sleep with)—well, Plan A is shot.

Depending on the disruption to Plan A, the passengers
may be clueless. If the plane isn't taking any sudden nose dives
or turns, the passengers are blissfully ignorant that their precious time on earth is coming to the end point. They have no
inkling that, yes, they should have purchased that American
Express Travel insurance—just $19.95 each time you fly—
guaranteeing surviving family members $1.5 million. They
have no clue that being rude and hostile and hanging up on the
telemarketing woman from American Express who bothered
them during dinner or petting their cat or watching television
or whatever it was that they were doing on some idle Tuesday
at 6 PM when she called was a big mistake.

"When four bells ring," he told me, "you're fucked."

I am a nervous flyer, but the good-looking flight attendant sitting next to me did not know this and so he told me about the four-bell system. We had bulkhead seats and he leaned back, stretching his legs and crossing them at the ankles. This was three years ago. We were en route to Miami, where I was going to visit my aunt and this off-duty flight attendant was going for a few days of R&R. The off-duty attendant was virtually hairless except for a perfectly quaffed, blond cut; he must have used gel or mousse or some sort of hair product because there was a glean to it, like an apple you just washed and are about to bite into. He was tan. His hands were perfectly manicured. And he swore to me—with a bit of lisp and downturning of long eyelashes—that he was not gay.

"Total stereotype that all male flight attendants are gay," he said, waving his hand back and forth as if dismissing a useless rumor, one not even worth passing on.

I didn't believe him. I didn't believe for one second that he wasn't gay. Either he was gay or he wanted to be or he dabbled on occasion.

I don't trust people. And this is the reason that I am a nervous flyer. I trust the theory of flight, the aerodynamics, the physics. I'm not overly concerned about clear-air wind sheers or flying into a flock of geese that clog up the engines. It's the people I don't trust: the engineer in charge of designing a fan belt who had a big blowout with his wife that morning and so he isn't paying attention to exactly how he is putting together this small and ever so significant part of the plane. The pilot who is addicted to Xanax and ran out and couldn't get any for three days because he doesn't have anybody to score from in St. Louis or Detroit or Burlington or whatever city he's flying out of and so he has begun to tremble uncontrollably; but he manages to score some Valium so he goes and takes a few too many Valium and now the trembling hands have ceased to tremble, because he's blitzed, completely stoned. The plane mechanic who was just diagnosed with liver cancer and he still has to tell his wife and two children and his mind is somewhere else—on the pain and the smell of hospitals and bile—and he forgets to put some piece of the plane machinery, some sort of plane widget, into its proper place during a maintenance check, and so not only is this mechanic going to die a horrible and bloated death, but so are you because the missing widget is going to cause a spiraling effect of systemic problems at 35,000 feet above the earth in a steel fuselage going almost 550 miles per hour.

There is no reason to trust anyone, not a single person involved in the whole creation and running of the plane and machinery, not the pilot or copilot, not the FAA, not the baggage handlers or air-traffic controllers, and certainly not the gay flight attendant who says he isn't gay. Trusting people is the greatest exercise in futility that we have in this world.

And although I didn't trust the flight attendant who was seated next to me—I believed him when he told me about the four-bell system on an airplane. I believed every word of this, because it was something that not only sounded true, but because it seemed almost a secret among all the personnel involved in the airline industry—a little factoid to keep unsuspecting passengers flying around the world. Keeping people misinformed—not religion—is the opiate of the masses.

⌒⅄⌒

I am on an airplane, a roomy 747, headed to the Frankfurt airport in Germany, where I am meeting my husband, Matthew. He is there for 12 days, for the Frankfurt Book Fair. He goes to the Book Fair every year, and every year I fly to Frankfurt toward the end of his trip to meet up with him, to take in the city a bit; after the Book Fair, we always head off to vacation for a while in France or Spain or Italy.

My husband, Matthew, is the Vice President and Publisher of Butterheim Longport Press, a gargantuan medical book publisher in Baltimore. Butterheim Longport has offices all over the world—Tokyo and London and Paris and Madrid. They are bigger than God. Matthew is only 42 years old, but he's just a few years from being CEO, from ruling the kingdom.

Matthew is cheating on me. He has been for nine months now. The girl—that's practically what she is, a girl, she's all of 25—whom he is fucking, is also in Frankfurt for the Book Fair. Matthew doesn't know I know—not that she is there in Frankfurt but that he is fucking her. Either he doesn't know that I know or his denial is so thick and impenetrable that he is blinded to my knowing. (Mostly I act like I don't know; it seems less real that way.) This girl he is fucking, and I use the term *fucking* because she is so young that that is all that it could possibly be, her name is Persephone. Persephone works with Matthew. She is an international rights manager. She sells translation rights to foreign publishers. With Persephone, you can publish your anatomy books in Turkish, your biology books in Greek, your immunology books in Portuguese, and your goddamn physiology books in Swahili. I know a lot about Persephone.

You'd know a lot about the woman your husband was fucking, too, if he was fucking her for nine months. You'd find out, you'd ask around, you'd call up another publishing company when you see an opening for an international rights manager in the classifieds and then you'd go interview for that job just to see what the girl who is fucking your husband does for eight hours a day.

Persephone and I met at the company Christmas party last year. She sought me out and introduced herself. This was my first clue about the affair. She was friendly, but demurely so, trying to be coy, I suspect. She told me she liked my dress. She told me twice—twice—how much she liked working with Matthew (she called him Matthew, not Matt like everyone else does, but Matthew) and I could tell by the way she spoke to me and the way she said his name—*Matthew*—that she had wrapped her cutesy, button-shaped mouth around his cock. It was all quite pathological in retrospect, her coming up to me and talking with me and engaging me like that—like the criminal returning to the crime scene, trying to look like a concerned citizen or curious passerby, but really only interested in watching the police try to gather all of the evidence.

Matthew and I live in a three-story farmhouse that was built in the 1850s—fireplace in the kitchen, nine bedrooms—on six acres of land outside of Annapolis. You can see the Severn River from our bedroom window. There used to be a barn on the property. Three of the barn walls were stone and the fourth wall and the roof were wood. I single-handedly—after we lost the twins—tore down the entire wood portion of the barn and left the three stone walls standing. Within what used to be the floor of the barn I created a garden. I've planted boxwood and hydrangea, and cutting flowers like peonies, black-eyed Susans, petunias, and day lilies. I've sectioned off an herb garden with basil, lemon thyme, English thyme, rosemary, oregano, and catmint. In the shady portion, I've put in hasta and a scattering of impatiens. Antique roses and wisteria crawl up the old stone walls. I care about this garden. I put my knees in the dirt. I water. I trim. I place human hair and bars of used soap in strategic locations in the garden during the height of July, when the deer are on their feeding warpath, to deter them.

I don't work. I was a senior underwriter for a mortgage insurance company. I quit six years ago, when I got pregnant with the twins. We don't need the money anyway. We can afford everything we want, and more, on Matthew's salary. I keep busy: I volunteer for the senior center. I exercise religiously; I have a washboard stomach and perfect legs and I can run the mile in 7 minutes and 12 seconds flat. I take classes at the local university—clay working, oil painting, introduction to graphics design, tai chi, Russian. I've leeched onto Russian. Someday I will read *Anna Karenina,* Rasputin, Gogol, Chekov, all in their native tongues. I'm on my fifth semester and it is tough, challenging. The pronunciations are nearly impossible—getting your tongue to hit a certain part of the roof of your mouth to make certain sounds. I am learning to speak Russian because I want to learn how to deal with difficult things.

I am missing Russian class this week so I can fly to Frankfurt to be with my cheating and lying husband whom I love, who loves me, who is there with Persephone, his lover. I've paid the next-door neighbor's kid—a gangly teenager named

Monica—to come over every day and water my garden that is surrounded by stone walls. It is August and everything, for now, is still blooming. If the garden isn't watered every day, it will fall apart. It will wither. It has to be watered in the early morning, before the sun has come out full force, so that the plants don't get scorched, so that they can quietly and calmly take in the water, absorb it all.

I hear the first ring. My heart skips a beat, like it always does. Then another ring. The captain comes on to tell us we're approaching a storm, that there will be turbulence, that the Fasten-Seatbelt light will be turned on. I hate turbulence. (I am wired and awake. I discovered last night that I am out of Ambien. Drinking through the flight won't help; alcohol makes me even more panicky, more claustrophobic. I am sober, alert. I have read the *International Herald Tribune, Entertainment Weekly*, the *Wall Street Journal*. I am abreast of what is going on in this world, in Hollywood, in the stock market. I am a well-informed woman.) The turbulence pushes at the plane. I feel like I'm on a ride at a traveling fair, the grimy and sleazy kind, where every ride shakes—the Twister, the Salt-n-Pepper Shaker, the Buccaneer. That is what it feels like, even in my $1,900 first-class seat.

The plane drops suddenly. Suddenly and far. I am in an aisle seat—7C—and the two seats on my left are empty. The first-class section is big; coach is ridiculously bigger. There's a shop—I'm not lying—a customs shop in coach, at the end of the plane, past row 52 or 53. The woman to my right is about 65 years old. She has red hair, a bad dye job with grayish-brown roots peaking from her scalp. She is short, thick around the middle, with little feet crammed into strappy shoes that look strained. She is scaldingly tan and she has a diamond on her left hand the size of a snowball—glistening and hard. She is reading a book—a thick and new romance novel. The turbulence and the sudden drop of altitude does not compel her to look at me for signs of reassurance or merely to share the fear or the surprise. She is unfazed. This is flying. This is life, I suppose she thinks.

And then another big drop in altitude, a low *whurrr* of the engine, and then more turbulence. (I suddenly make a decision about God: I believe in him. I do. I really think I do.) I ignore that sound I think that I'm hearing from the left side of the plane. I am always hearing a sound. I dig in the seat pocket for the headphones. A movie is on: *Forrest Gump*. I've seen it already, twice. But the sound is making me nervous, so is the way the plane is bouncing, so I will watch the movie. For the third time. One, two, three *Forrest Gump*s.

And right before I put the headphones on—I'm just sliding the well-sanitized headpiece over my ears—I hear the overhead bell. One ring. Then two. Another announcement from the cockpit? Then the third. A cup of coffee for the pilot? And then there it is. Stop. There it is. Magic number four. One, two, three, four.

Everything stops in my head and chest and heart. Fear seizes, clutches at me, freezing me, and framed in the panic of my vision is everyone, here on this plane, crystallizing into shaved ice.

⌒⫟⌒

Our sleek and silky first-class flight attendant has slithered away, headed north, toward the cockpit with stealth and not an eyebrow raised. Four bells have rung—maybe two messages from the pilot. Two double rings in a row. Maybe it means we're getting two messages. Two plus two is four. I want more.

The pilot comes on the overhead speaker. "I'm going to take us up to 40,000 feet and try to get above the storm," he says. "I'd like to remind everyone at this time that the Fasten-Seatbelt sign is lit. For your safety, please remain in your seats with your seatbelt fastened securely. Thank you."

The goddamn pilot is lying and I know it. This is a bona fide, Class A, number 1 lie. A lie is the easiest thing in the world to detect, but the reason lying works so well is not because the liar is a good liar. Most liars, except for the truly disturbed, are pretty lousy at myth making and truth raping. The reason a lie works so well is because of the absolute weakness and stupidity of the person being lied to. This is my take. Sorry, I blame the victim.

A flight attendant from coach has just sauntered up into first class. She smiles at me and keeps moving forward toward the front of the plane. She waltzes through the forest-green curtain that separates first class from the short walkway to the cockpit. I know the pilot who came over the loudspeaker was lying because of his voice—the barely perceptible crack, the forced nature, the affected sense of calm. Any half-brain would recognize the lie. There is a woman in coach, I can hear her, but just faintly. She is hysterical. She is hysterical and there isn't a flight attendant to be found. That woman back in coach—the only voice I can hear—is one smart cookie.

The pilot lied. This is not about turbulence. This is not just a bad storm. I want to walk through that forest-green curtain and barge in on the pow-wow going on between the cockpit crew and the flight attendants trying to figure out how to save us. I want to call them on their lie. I want to confront them. I want them to understand that no matter what, this is not acceptable. I want the truth and I want an apology from the lying pilot and the glistening flight attendants wearing the lie on their sleeves. Life just trickles down to a bunch of near misses and half-truths and good intentions and plenty of apologies, given and taken. I have so many apologies. I want one from the pilot. Now. I want an apology for the lie (is there time?) and for now all I can do—all I will do—is make my own apology (you are sorry, very sorry, when four bells ring), and this is no lie: I am sorry for the two abortions. They were wrong. I did the wrong thing. Matthew and I did the wrong thing because we were selfish and young and inconvenienced. Matthew only knows about the first one. The second one was three months before our wedding. And I couldn't tell him. I fought all of the inconveniences tooth and nail and I won. I took two babies—I snatched them. And then six years later, I was pregnant with twins. Twins. One baby, two baby—for me and Matthew. And then at eight months, they stopped moving. One day it all got quiet in the swell of my stomach and our twins were dead ("An intrauterine infection. Very rare," the doctors said). Two I took. Two were taken. One, two (I lied), three, four, all dead. Four dead babies and I apologize. I swear to God I am so sorry.

Lies beget lies, which beget apologies, making room for forgiveness, moving onto more lies. Elliot, the man who was my lover for five years before I met Matthew was an expert liar.

(You think about old lovers and old lies when you are on a plane that rang four bells.) The lying was in his name, something I discovered during a game of anagrams: The name *Elliot* can make the words *lie lot*. He lied alot. My Elliot, the *lie lot* boy. And it is only now, after the four rings, that I can forgive him. I finally forgive him. I do. One, two, three, four, forgive.

For Elliot, the truth (that he loved another man more than he loved me) was a heavy, incomprehensible stone in his throat that he couldn't clear. So he loved me as hard as he could. He held me. He begged me to sleep in the nude so he could wrap his naked body around mine and in our vulnerable nakedness the truth couldn't get to us. We were like babies—we were, a pack of puppies snuggled together, needing something, having to fend for ourselves eventually. I forgive him for lying to me. (Because I let him lie. I helped him lie. I nursed and coddled and fondled the lies. If the lie was there, we could be together, and I loved him impossibly. I loved him more than he loved the man whom he lied to me for: a gray and wrinkled philosophy professor named Max.)

I wish I was more. I wish I wasn't on this plane. I wish I could have told Elliot so many years ago not to lie. I wish I could have halted the first lie he told me: that he was getting 12 credits toward his graduate degree to spend four weeks traveling through Southeast Asia with Max, the gray professor. (He wasn't getting 12 credits. He was just traveling for four weeks through Southeast Asia with Max. He left out the part that he was fucking Max and inserted the 12 credits.) I wish I could have stopped that lie and then spared so many others.

I wish I could have stopped myself from getting on this plane. This plane that shakes. A flight attendant has broken from the pack near the cockpit and is making her way back to coach, probably to see to the hysterical woman, who is still hysterical. I swear I can hear a hysterical woman back there in coach, away from the comfort of first class.

I wish that when Matthew called me at noon yesterday—7 PM Frankfurt time (was he getting ready for dinner with Persephone?)—that I would have said to him, I'm not coming to Germany. I wish I would have asked him how Persephone is, if she is that good of a fuck to be still fucking her after nine months. But here I am and this is where I have let Matthew's lie take me. I wish I would have just stayed in the house this morning and missed the plane. I wish I would have strapped myself into my home. Then I wouldn't have to be on this plane with the four rings. I would be tending to my garden, drinking iced tea on our porch, learning Russian, difficult things.

This was what I am now convinced was my last supper: a not-so-bad breast of chicken with herbs, asparagus with no crunch to it, warm sourdough rolls slathered in butter, a diet coke, and an apple fritter. I consumed this, all of this, before the four bells rang. The plane is still shaking and I'm about to vomit all over myself. I'm about to puke up my last supper. Fuck this. Just absolutely fuck this.

My mother is dead: three years ago, complications of diabetes. My father is dead: 17 years ago, massive coronary. My four babies are dead. My sister is alive and kicking: She has three children and a husband I love as if he was my own flesh-and-blood brother. I have a husband: He's busy fucking a 25-year-old, but I love him.

I'm pissed off that I didn't change the will after he started with Persephone (but I couldn't, you see—he'd know I knew). Everything of mine, the 401k, a $500,000 life insurance policy, all of it will go to the lying husband that I love, and then he and Persephone can live happily ever after in my house and wake up every morning and walk into the kitchen that I painted, the Arts and Crafts furniture that I picked out, the garden that I took care of—the life that I planted.

We should prepare for these things better. For dying and death and the suddenness of it. For plane crashes. Really, we should be ready for this shit. Not so our loved ones are all taken care of and the life insurance policy is worked out, but we should have given and accepted apologies, forgiven grievances, called the liars on their lies.

I am pissed that the statistics are coming home. How am I to call my losses and walk away? This—being in a plane that rang four bells (that is in trouble, that is going down) and wondering what goes through all the passengers' minds—this is the shit that I randomly think about in the middle of one of those days when I am saddened by everything I see.

(I feel like I see everything on sad days: the old man standing at the corner of a busy intersection waiting for a bus that isn't coming because the bus stop is two blocks away, but you and no one else bothers to do anything about it [you couldn't if you wanted to—you are in your car, you are stuck in traffic] and you aren't going to turn around at the next intersection and go back and be inconvenienced just for some old man who looks a little lost. [But you know he is. He is lost.] The same day you see a woman in front of you in the checkout line at the grocery store and she is in one of those motor-powered wheelchairs and you can tell that she is wearing a wig and she is so thin and she is your age and you know it must be breast cancer or ovarian cancer or something like that and her husband is with her and so is her son who looks about nine or ten and they are all trying to just live their lives in this death dance that they are on.)

On those days, those sad days, I think about what a passenger in a plane that is going down must be thinking about. Do they pray to God? Do they hold the hand of the person next to them?

(There is no one next to me on my left. And I can't hold that red-haired woman's hand. She is still reading her romance novel. She doesn't think anything is wrong. She doesn't know about the four-bell system.)

"Ladies and Gentleman," the captain announces. He has returned.

"We'd like to apologize for the continued inconveniences associated with the heavy turbulence we are experiencing. Going up to 40,000 feet hasn't helped much, but maybe a little. We should be out of this storm's way within about 20 minutes or so."

We are going down and this captain is still lying to us. I've had enough of all of this. You see, men have been lying to me my whole life and it's going to stop right this very second. It will stop now. I am not going to leave this mediocre life of mine with the last man who talks to me lying. It won't happen. I won't let it happen.

The flight attendant from first class, Amanda, that is her name, Amanda—she must be senior supervisor flight attendant or something; she's got special wings on her uniform and has an air of command. She has presence. She's back from coach, where I know I heard a woman sobbing. (I know I heard the cries of a woman back there.) That is why senior flight attendant Amanda probably had to go back to coach, to control the hysterical woman, to make the passengers feel like everything is really okay. And now she's back to serving us; all 30 of us in a big first-class section where I'm the only one who has any clue as to what is going on in this plane, in this world, it seems. She is talking in her flight attendant tone of calm chipperness to the elderly couple two rows ahead of me. She is telling them about some cathedral in Frankfurt. I see through the veneer of her sprayed hair and tiny waist and the capped teeth and the smile that goes with it. I see right through all of this and I can't just sit here anymore.

I can't just sit here, fastened to this seat, to this place, to someone else's Plan B. I unhook my seatbelt. It is the sound of metal against metal, but it's a releasing sound. I'm letting go of all of this. The woman next to me looks up from her paperback novel; the plane is shaking and her attention is directed right at me. For the first time since four bells rang, the woman with the red hair and the gold jewelry looks concerned. She is watching me. She is about to say something. I stand up, and heads are turning. The plane drops suddenly— as if me standing up has weighed it down some, forced the gravity of these situations upon the steel and board—and I am ready to walk out of my seat and go to the cockpit and tell them I know all about the four rings.

I can feel senior flight attendant Amanda moving toward me. She is making her way toward me. To stop me.

"Can I help you?" she says, her hand reaching out toward me.

"Can I help you?"

OUTCOMES

I saw him for just a brief glimpse. In a flash, like the bright blink-and-pop of a flash cube, the kind you'd attach to the top of your 110-millimeter camera: He was sitting on the toilet seat, not taking a shit or anything, just sitting there. He was wearing a pair of charcoal-gray sweatpants and a matching sweatshirt, something that looked recently purchased, something that hid the wasting of his body, a wasting that had reached the point of me walking through his front door. Me, the home health aid from the hospice, who had come to give him a sponge bath.

I had called out his name, Lawrence, when I first walked through the cramped and musty living room of his apartment on Argyle Street, in the King's Cross section of London. Lawrence didn't answer. I saw a light coming from the end of the hall. Maybe he was in the bathroom. I got a quick knot, a flurry, a grumbling of the bowels. Maybe he was on the toilet having trouble taking a shit, or was losing so much shit that he was too weak to get up and wipe himself.

The glimpse: The gun was raised to his temple, but slightly askew, his hand trembling, the defeated and tired look on his face of *Please just leave me alone.* My hand raised upward—to my mouth to cover it? to the crossing guard position of *Stop?* I don't know. And then he pulled the trigger, an eardrum-shattering sound, and then it just blew away—half of his head flew in bits and pieces in one direction across the bathroom, hitting the ceiling and splattering the periwinkle walls. A darkness, from his blood, spread across the top of his sweatshirt and his whole body slumped to the left and fell off the white porcelain toilet. There was a distinct clonk as his wrist hit the clean metal pipes of the stand-alone sink.

Lawrence was my first patient, on the first day of my new job. This was the first dying patient that I was tending to. I ran to the living room, picked up the phone and dialed 911, forgetting my instructions from orientation, forgetting for a moment that I was in London, where 911 wasn't the answer to a crisis.

I moved from Philadelphia to England three months ago with my fiancé, Sanjay. He was granted a two-year special residency in the Microbiology and Immunology Department at the Princess Grace Hospital in London. Sanjay is a second-year resident in infectious disease. He is obsessed with the bug parade: *Klebsiella pneumoniae, Clostridium perfringens, Shigella dysenteriae, Mycobacterium tuberculosis, Streptococcus pyogenes.* He's been shoving his eye into the lens of a microscope since his junior year in high school, trying to figure out how the things we can't see can hurt us so much.

We met two years ago. I was working as an editor for the *Journal of Microbiology and Infectious Disease*. Sanjay wrote an article on the burgeoning strains of antibiotic-resistant *Salmonella* species. He's a lousy writer, and I gave his article a much needed butcher job. He called me when it published and reamed me a new asshole, telling me I had no right to do what I did. Just who the hell did I think I was, he asked. I was used to this, the arrogance of these doctors and scientists. You wouldn't believe it.

"If you think for one second that you can talk to me like that, then your inability to write a complete sentence is only the beginning of your problems," I spit at him after his tirade. I had made unprofessional leaps before, but not like that. He called me the next day to apologize.

"I want to convince you that I'm really not one of those egotistical doctors, I just sometimes accidentally act like one," he said. Months later, when we were together and in love, he told me it was that moment—when I leaped—that he fell in love with me.

When we got to London, I started to look for a job. I had to get a job to get a work visa, and the paperwork involved was overwhelming: form after form to be completed, signatures to be had by every imaginable bureaucrat in England and the United States. And the job market in London was horrible. These were my choices: waitress, clerk, waitress, clerk, waitress, clerk. None of it was anything that I wanted. And the truth was, I didn't know what I wanted anymore. I was 30 years old, tired of being an editor, and convinced that the whole career thing was overrated anyway. The eighties ruined it for women. We're expected to want everything, to want to wear high-power, expensive suits and crash through glass ceilings and climb corporate ladders, all while nurturing a marriage, having a suckling infant at our breast, and serving up dinner every evening. Screw that.

What I want, what I really want, is a baby. I want to have a baby. But we're not ready yet—that is, Sanjay isn't ready yet. We get married next year, but we've got the two years in London before he goes on to a fellowship. Sanjay wants us to wait at least four years, which seems like forever, before we start a family. I'm paranoid that I won't be able to have a baby. Sanjay doesn't know about this fear, and he doesn't know that since I boarded the plane to London, I ceased and desisted taking birth control. I threw my packet of Ortho Tri-Cyclen into the waste bin in the bathroom of the British Airways 757 we were on.

A baby boy is what I'd really like. I want a boy as beautiful as Sanjay. I want boys, like Princess Diana had—two of them, one sweet and one sort of devilish. I'm a bit fascinated with Princess Di. She may be dead, but there is still plenty to follow, especially here in England. Her face still graces almost every major tabloid. Her childhood home, the estate of Althorp, just an hour north of London, is open to the public for tours this summer. Tickets are scarce, basically impossible to get ahold of. I told Sanjay that being a doctor is a waste of time if he doesn't put his connections to good use.

"All right, Rena, I'll make a deal with you. I'll see about getting you some tickets to this Althorp place, but you have to go on an interview for a job I just heard about."

"What kind of job did you hear about?" I asked.

"A home health aide job. Marty over in oncology told me about it."

I think Sanjay was getting worried that I still hadn't gotten a job. That I'd turned into some lazy fiancé and was just a few months away from permanent unemployment, weight gain, and an obsession with bad television.

"It's for some hospice near Euston Station," he said. "Basically, you tend to the dying. And you'd be qualified, of course."

"Sanjay, I was a nursing assistant for one year when I was 19. I don't know if that qualifies me for much."

"It's a home health aide job, not head nurse."

I decided to check it out. Out of curiosity more than anything. I am forever curious about the human body—its parts, its functions, and its never ending variety of dysfunctions. This curiosity is what brought me to and kept me in medical publishing for so long. Disease captivates me, from the autoimmune to the infectious to the lifestyle-induced to the genetically inevitable to those of unknown origin. There is no end to the list of things that can go wrong for us in this world.

"Just go interview. Trust me, you don't need to worry much about messing up when working for a hospice," he said. "The outcome is always the same."

"You have some experience, and I think you can handle this," Bridget, the nurse manager at the hospice, said. "But you should know," she said, getting serious and looking me straight in the eye, "I honestly believe that this kind of work is a calling."

"You mean like priesthood?" I asked. And then I was immediately worried that I sounded cavalier, even though I didn't mean to.

"Yes, exactly. This is more than the nursing assistant work you did. Hospice is more than just a job."

And my heart sunk when she said this, because really, that's all I wanted, was a job. I didn't want a career. I wanted a job and a baby—I wanted the living. I wanted to embrace the living, but I was settling for just a job, with the dying. And she was telling me it was more than that. I didn't have the calling, but I had the qualifications, and I showed enough of what Bridget wanted to see to get me the job. And Sanjay wanted me to have a job, so I took it.

A home health aide does a bit of everything for the dying patient: sponge baths, changing bedsheets, cleaning bed pans, propping up pillows. You wash their hair or just comb it for them and put a barrette in it, you shave their beard, trim a mustache. You help them out around the house, running the vacuum and watering the plants, or fetching them a book or magazine or glass of juice. You make small talk, or big talk, depending on the patient's mood, desire, or morphine dosage. You try to gauge whether the patient wants to chat, wants to talk seriously about what was going on in a swirl around them, or doesn't want you to say anything and simply wants to be. And finally, you have to know CPR, but you never have to use it. Almost all hospice patients have chosen to be DNR—Do Not Resuscitate. There's no need to stop the inevitability of the end.

⸎

The guy who shot himself—Lawrence Bartholomew—was DNR. Lying between his sink and his toilet with a gunshot wound through his head. The dying man who seized his own death before it could seize him. AIDS was his intended end. But endings can change, even at the final moment.

I shook. That was all I could do in that moment, with the smell of a fired gun, my ears hurting, and the sight of this dead dying man slumped in his bathroom. I shook. Lawrence's brother had been in the laundry room at the other end of the apartment building, and he ran back when he heard the shot. And when he saw Lawrence, he just started screaming. I did not know what to do. When I was in orientation and going to a patient's home with a senior nurse, I saw nothing like this. I was in an apartment on my first official day of my new job with a dead man on his bathroom floor and his screaming, howling brother.

As the police and paramedics were leaving, two guys from the morgue came. I could hear their playful banter as they walked into the apartment. They were young, with pasty skin, thick Cockney accents, dyed hair in spiky punk rocker cuts, facial piercings. But they were all business when they entered the bathroom and saw what they saw. They became quiet and went about their work with a grace reserved only, I thought, for saints and old people.

"Be careful," I said, when I was leading them toward the bathroom. "He had AIDS, so be careful, you know, the blood and everything."

"Yeah, we know," the shortest one said. "Protocol to always wear protective gear."

I went and sat on the couch, to shake, to wait. I had already called Bridget, and she had asked me to stay there with Lawrence's brother. Bridget was sending Margaret, a supervisor, over to help out, and she wanted me to stick around until Margaret arrived. Someone was going to have to clean up the bathroom when the morgue guys were done. Someone from the hospice was going to have to take care of what was next.

"Not you," Bridget told me, calming me with her soothing voice. "I don't want you to clean that up. You've had enough for one day. But I need you to stay there, okay, until Margaret gets there. Is that okay?"

"Yeah. I can stay," I said, my voice shaking like my hands. "No problem."

I sat there on the couch, picking at my fingernails and twirling my engagement ring, an emerald-cut diamond in an antique platinum setting, looking around the room, surveying it, taking in the living room of a dead man whose family, at that moment, were just getting the news that he was dead. The intimacy of what I already knew and what they didn't struck me, because I was just a stranger.

And then I saw a glimmer of silver. A shine on the coffee table. I moved closer. Tickets. I picked them up, held them in my hands. Two tickets on a sky-blue onion paper, the size of a check, with a silver overlay in the middle, shiny and smooth. The overlay was the Spencer family coat of arms; engraved in the overlay was *Althorp*.

Two tickets to Princess Diana's childhood home. To her burial place. At the bottom of the ticket was a date and time: 14 July 1998, 10:00 AM. Two tickets that cost only nine pounds each—about 15 US dollars—but were priceless in a way, impossible to get ahold of. And before I could think or stop or pause or question any rights or wrongs or moral ambiguities, I put the tickets in my brown leather purse. I heard in the background the swoosh of the morgue guys putting Lawrence's ended life in a bag. And then they walked down the hall with the bag, past me, toward the door. And there I was, witness to it all.

From that first day when Lawrence shot himself and I took the tickets to Althorp, I began to steal something whenever I walked into the home of a patient who was going to die during my visit. I stole something to keep it all consistent for me, to keep the people who died and the deaths that I witnessed, with me. To find a person dead, or to be a witness to their death, is important. It means something. It must be marked for the person who is alive, who is a witness, with more than a prayer or sympathy card or showing up at the funeral, which is what we do at the hospice to show our support to the family. Something more is needed for the one who gets to live and was there to see the living go from living to dead. There is a connection when you witness this. So I take something. Something small. Something that will go unnoticed. I don't steal jewelry or appliances or silver candlesticks or any family heirloom. I take a tie tack, a coffee mug, a gaudy fake-jewel-encrusted hair clip, a bottle of perfume.

I took a light blue, gauzy Italian scarf from a 47-year-old history professor who succumbed to amyotrophic lateral sclerosis. She went into respiratory failure and died during my visit with her. Her husband was grocery shopping and missed it all.

I took a dog-eared Ronaldo soccer card from a 56-year-old man who died after the irrepressible tumor in his lung grew up and away through his system, causing superior vena cava syndrome and a host of other complications. For the few weeks before he died, I witnessed how his face swelled, how his eyes seemed more and more bugged out every time I saw him, even though the skin and flesh around his body grew thinner and tighter. When I got there for my thrice-weekly appointment, the family was huddled around him and Rosemary, one of the hospice nurses, was already there. Rosemary and I stayed with the family and held hands with them. His wife sang quietly to him as he went on to wherever it is that we go.

I took a small tile, hand painted in Mexico, from a 64-year-old widow whose organs failed as kidney disease finished its job. The mantel of her fireplace was lined with different-size tiles—in hues of red and burnt sienna and cobalt blue—which she had collected from her travels all over the world. The tile I took was small enough to fit in the palm of my hand, painted in a sea-green floral design with fits and bursts of sun-yellow splotches. I chose my piece of her that I wanted to take with me. Even though she was mean and nasty and never found a moment of grace in her dying, the fact that I was there when she died could not go unnoticed.

I took the tile because she was dead and it's always the same, this ritual: We all die, we all die alone, we all die differently, and if I'm there when they die, I take something of theirs from this world. Because it's all the same anyway.

⌒⁂⌒

There is something very living about watching the dying. You force yourself to slow down, to go with that moment and relinquish control. You just do your tasks and stand there with each patient and take full recognition of the present moment. So as messy as it can be, my job isn't stressful in the conventional sense of stressful. I've made a friend in one of the nurses, Rosemary. I love her biting edge and forthright nature, all of which is mixed with this undeniable tenderness. She is the kind of nurse I'd want if I was dying: funny as hell and gifted at subsiding the fear a dying person can have.

"I was convinced you were a goner," Rosemary said. She was talking about my first day on the job.

"You were?" I asked.

"Well, yeah. A dying man goes and bloody well blows his brains out in front of you? I was convinced that your first day was also your last."

"Well, it was *full-blown* AIDS, you know," I said, deadpan.

"Shit," Rosemary said, her shoulders bouncing as she tried to stifle a laugh. You laugh a lot in hospice about things that aren't funny. Without sick jokes, without obnoxious puns, and without eliminating *Time* from the infamous *Tragedy* + *Time* = *Comedy* equation, I'd be overwhelmed. There is a comfort in the irony, a sense of control. And a sense that you are protected too.

"I never worry about getting cancer," Rosemary said to me one day.

"You don't?" I asked.

"Hell no. Hospice nurses can't get cancer," she said with certainty. "God wouldn't let that shit happen to us."

And you start to believe in God, some God, any God. Something. Because something like dying to happen so slowly has to be explained, understood. Something. Whether we came in as Protestants, Catholics, Jews, Buddhists, Jehovah's Witnesses, Scientologists, agnostics, or atheists, we all walk out of the hospice's main office at the end of the day and get on the crowded Tube, where nobody talks to each other, and we have a secret inside; we know there is a God.

"Guess what I got?" Rosemary asked me, in a sing-songy voice. We were in the office picking up our schedules.

"What?" I asked, thinking she was going to announce a new car or a puppy.

"Two tickets to Althorp," she said, so excited that she was almost smug.

"How did you get them?" I asked, feigning interest, out of a sense of shame more than anything. My two tickets were warming a spot in my underwear drawer, and I was still planning to go, alone, of course. I hadn't told anyone about them.

"Oh, my husband got them through someone at his office. I have to take my sister because her birthday is coming up and she'd just kill me if I took anyone else, you know. Oh, Rena, you know I'd love to take you with me," she said, her heavy London accent sounding even heavier with her sincerity.

"Rosemary, stop. I'd never expect you take me. I mean thanks for thinking of me and everything, but you don't have to explain," I said, forcing a grin and feeling my secret welling up in me.

"I saw Nancy today," I said, changing the subject and pushing the image of Lawrence and the tickets back to the place where I was keeping them.

"I just saw her on Monday," Rosemary said. "She's a tough one to go to, eh? So young and everything, and having that little baby of hers and all. Oh I've been praying like mad to God, more than usual, for her to go quick."

"I got to hold her baby for a while today. She's such a beautiful baby," and I feel my heart slip toward that warmth.

"Nancy doesn't have much time," Rosemary said, "I can just feel it, you know. Two weeks tops I'd say."

Nancy is a patient that haunts me. She fills my dreams at night sometimes. And I dream a lot about her 8-month-old baby, Georgia. Nancy is my age and she has so much. She has a loving husband and this baby girl. She was right in the middle of this perfect life: a new baby, a lovely home, and a wonderful husband. And then she couldn't get past the shoulder pain that had plagued her throughout her pregnancy, and then some tests, and then a diagnosis: a truly rare and unexplainable occurrence of pancreatic cancer. Already spread, death being the only end in sight. This was going to take her to her next life, just as her new baby was beginning hers.

It is difficult to go to Nancy's, to bathe her, to tend to her. The unfairness of it is closer than I want it to be. It is a dying I have trouble with. It is not what you see in the movies or on television. None of it in hospice ever is. In the face of the dying, the inevitability, it lacks all the melodrama you assume will be there. It's just scary and out of control, but feels frighteningly natural. Nancy haunts me because she is dying of something that just happened to her, not because of a lifetime of poor health or overconsumption of all those wonderful bad things like cigarettes and alcohol and fatty foods. Not that you want the lung cancer patients who smoked all their lives or the diabetic patients who never followed their prescribed diets to die—you don't—and you don't blame them for their illness per se. But patients who get bad luck or have a shitty gene pool and wake up one day terminally ill are the hardest cases to witness.

When I go to Nancy's, I bring something with me. Sometimes I bring a rattle or stuffed animal for Georgia. Her darling baby who has porcelain skin and these big blue eyes that look right up at you. I love to hold Georgia. Babies are miracles to me.

Nancy smiles weakly, but genuinely, when I come to her house. Last week I brought her a Philadelphia Phillies baseball hat. Nancy has never been to the United States, and she loves that I'm an American, is sort of fascinated with my accent. I like to tease with her and exaggerate the harshness of a Philly accent. She laughs, as if I am imitating someone other than myself.

It is hard to take the baby from Nancy's arms when I am visiting. Nancy cries when I bathe her. Not because I am hurting her, but because it is time that she isn't touching her baby. The dying are smarter than the rest of us. They make us feel dumb and ungrateful and clumsy and they humble us to the largeness of something like holding a baby.

On July 14, the day for Althorp, I got my period. The same period I've been having since I was 13. Heavy on the first day. Light on the second day. Practically gone on the third. I cried while sitting on the toilet, my pajamas at my feet. The shower was running, so Sanjay couldn't hear me. I keep getting it. My period is an overplayed song on the radio that I'm so sick of hearing but that I sing along to anyway because I can't help myself.

Since that day on the plane when I threw out my pills, it's been only Sanjay and me when we make love. Just the two of us and our biologies and chemistries and nothing has happened. I get scared that Sanjay and I are destined to be only that: Sanjay and I. That we will have only a house and nice cars and maybe a dog or two and a lush garden that I can tend to, but that I will not be able to have kids.

July 14. An American in Althorp. Four months since I walked in on Lawrence Bartholomew sitting in his AIDS-weakened state, blowing his brains out. My first day in hospice. My first death. My first dead person's possession and now here I was, bringing it to full circle, going to see the beautiful dead Princess's home.

I take the Tube from the Highgate station, only a few blocks from where we live. Highgate is hip, expensive, and lined with boutiques, pubs, and beauty salons where for 65 pounds you can get some waiflike and arrogant guy, who looks like a girl, to trim your hair into a fashionable cut. On my way to the Tube, I pass Highgate Cemetery, a huge resting place for wealthy Londoners, not to mention a slew of the famous: the writer George Eliot, who is buried under her real name, Mary

Ann Evans; Karl Marx; the poet Christina Rossetti; Henry Gray, the anatomist of *Gray's Anatomy;* and the famous social Darwinist Herbert Spencer. I like to walk around the cemetery and read the graves, see how old the people were when they died. Entrance to the cemetery is one pound 20 pence. The middle-age lady with frizzy gray hair who collects the entrance fee knows me. She knows I'm a regular, not a tourist, so she's stopped charging me.

"I like to look at all the graves, too. So quiet, you know? The dead are so quiet. That's why I like my job so much. I like the quiet," she said. I had come by last week after work to walk around.

"Yes," I said, "all that quiet must be nice."

"They all had such different lives, didn't they? But here they are now, in the same place."

"Yeah," I said, "the outcome is always the same."

"You know," she told me, "I know how the famous ones here died. Karl Marx, George Eliot—"

She paused in a slow way, grasping her own words, stopping herself.

"Oh, Jesus Mary and Joseph, you must think I'm a bloody nut," she said, giggling and a bit flushed.

"No, no," I said to her, assuring her she's not a nut. "I think about dying all the time."

I take the Northern Line to Euston Station, and then get on the Victoria Line and take it to the St. Pancras Station, the same stop I got off the day I saw Lawrence's end. From St. Pancras I take a British Rail Line out of London, on to Northampton. A bus service was arranged to bring people from the Northampton station to Althorp, so as not to upset the neighboring homes of equally aristocratic English families by having the masses parking cars along their idyllic country lanes.

When I get off the train at Northampton, there is already a line of people waiting at a queue to board an Althorp-bound double-decker bus. The line is full of British women, dressed in their Sunday best, most of them carrying fresh flowers. I board the bus, pay the two-pound fare, and take a seat in the front row of the upper deck. Everything seems dangerously close at this seat. Telephone lines, traffic lights, and tree branches feel as if they will come through the window and land on your lap like an unintended gift.

We drive through the opened and massive wrought-iron gates of the estate down a narrow one-lane road. A tour guide is waiting as we get off the bus. He is a white-haired man with a dignified London accent and a navy blazer with the Althorp coat of arms on the breast. He points across the lane to the nearly 500-year-old house, welcoming in the living. He tells us that we can tour the first floor of the house, and we can follow the dirt path to the island where the Princess is buried. And then he points toward the stables, where there are two small buildings set up exhibiting some of Diana's famous wardrobe, including her wedding dress, as well as a sampling of her child-hood effects, and a display of sympathy cards and condolence books. Finally, there is a gift shop.

We get to walk through Althorp unguided and at our own pace, like we are a family friend visiting. But there is a gift shop, isn't there? So the feeling-like-a-family-friend is just a well-con-structed facade that I see through. How are we to honor the dead? Rich or poor or worshiped or forgotten or loved or hated, how do we honor them?

I walk toward her home, her childhood place, her resting place, her memorials. What could I see? You see only a one-dimensional still-frame once a person is dead. You see more when they are dying than when they are dead. I saw her grave. I saw her childhood living room, backyard, and gardens. I saw her condolence books and the displays of sympathy cards sent. One of them, made by an eight-year-old boy from Yorkshire, was a drawing of a rainbow with a sun and an angel in the sky and written at the bottom of the light blue construction-paper card—*Every end is a new beginning.* I saw a glimpse of her life.

And later, feeling tired and crampy and let down somehow, expecting a dead Princess's home to be something more, I saw Rosemary. I was back on the bus, in the same seat, at the top and front. There was Rosemary. An electric wave of panic struck me, like a shock from putting your finger in an open socket. I saw Rosemary getting off a bus, which was bringing the afternoon ticket holders. There she was. *She is almost a friend,* I thought. I felt caught.

Rosemary turned around with her sister to listen to the same tour guide give the same speech. She was facing me, directly, and she had her hand up as a visor over her eyes, to keep the sun from shining right in them. All she had to do was look up a bit, just a bit, to see me. And she did. She looked up. I could swear she looked right at me, but it was hard to tell, with her hand up over her eyes shielding them from the sun. She looked right at me, but I don't know if she saw me.

The next day my period was still coming heavily. More heavily than normal. Big strange clots of blood rested in the toilet after I peed. I called Sanjay and he told me not to worry, teased me that I was a hypochondriac, reminded me that the body isn't perfect.

"Call in sick," he says, "if you feel that bad."

But I couldn't call in sick. It is Wednesday, and I am scheduled to go to Nancy's house; I always go to Nancy's house on Wednesdays. I wash her hair on Wednesdays. I've been bringing a scented shampoo from my own collection at home. I have a huge array of soaps and salves and gels and washes, in scents of kiwi and apricot and chamomile and wildflower. I am soothed by smells, by the floral and the citrus and the fruity. Nancy likes them, too. She tries to guess what the scent is—a different one each visit—after I begin to gently lather her thin hair.

I didn't want to go to Nancy's that morning. There's part of me that never, never wants to go to Nancy's. But it is harder not to go than to just go. Who would want to go? To see what she has? And what she soon won't? It is too much of life to witness. After going to Nancy's house I think too much, everything becomes otherworldly, as if it is not only her life slipping away. I could flip burgers, type memos, edit manuscripts, or tend to the dying. But either way, it leaves me saddened by the world.

It is a stereotype of a London day— misty rain and dark and cold. I walk into Nancy's house and there are about ten or eleven people in the living room and kitchen, moving about the house. This is not unusual, to walk into a full house. It's either full or nearly empty, because family and friends will either altogether avoid or gravitate to the dying. I see a young-looking woman, lithe and blonde. She is carrying baby Georgia, doing a walk that is at once a slow saunter and a bounce, a bouncy walk. Babies like that bouncy sensation. I don't know who this young girl is—maybe Nancy's sister. I try to see some resemblance, but I only know what Nancy looks like as a dying person. And someone who is dying stops looking like their healthy former selves; they become a ghost human.

Bridget is in the hallway, huddled with Nancy's husband, Hugh, and Nancy's mother. Bridget turns and sees me and gives me her warm smile. Bridget does that—she warms you up and calms you down and brings the atmosphere to a cottony softness, even in the middle of dying people and suffering families.

I've learned that people die at different paces. Some go on a steady and gradual downhill slope that is barely perceptible if you see them regularly. Some go much more quickly, just flying down the tube toward the end. Some people stair-step: They seem to be doing good one day, then horrible the next day, then good again the next day (but not as good as the other day), then bad again. Rosemary and I talked early in the week about how Nancy was actively dying—a hospice term that is both an oxymoron and a perfect description of how our lives take on reliable patterns toward the end. There are predictable signs of active dying: The patient is bed bound, less aware of their surroundings; they have a signature breathing pattern. And they often exhibit "communication of the dying"—they have unexplainable conversations with dead relatives, they speak out about being ready or mutter *I can go home now,* they lay there clueless that you and all of their family are in the room but their eyes are wide open staring at the ceiling, their arms reaching skyward, aware of something.

And because Bridget is here, not scheduled to be here, but now here, I know that not only is Nancy actively dying but she is very close to the end.

"Do you want to stick around?" Bridget asks me. "I know the family could really use the support."

"Yeah, sure," I reply. "Of course," and I say this firmly now. I am a witness. How can I move from this place?

I mill around the house, talking with people. With everyone else who is here for Nancy's death. Here to witness. I have begun to get comfortable with how to talk with the families. I speak in a soft voice that is almost breathy and puts a person at ease. I have found that speaking softly and saying very little is the best kind of support.

I need to go upstairs. I've washed Nancy's hair in scents of mangoes and lavender and older flowers. I've held her baby. I've held her hand. It is the right thing to do, to go see the dying to whom you have tended. You just move past all that makes you feel uncomfortable. You learn to shepherd your way.

"The only difference between the dying and yourself," Bridget told me when I started this job, "is they basically know when and how their life will end, whereas the rest of us are still in denial about dying altogether."

I go upstairs. Nancy looks horrible. She is gray and yellow and she can't swallow food and she can't even speak any more and her face is drawn, and yet she is not ugly. She is alive; and here are all of us, thriving, shepherding. I put my hand on her arm and touch her lightly; her peach-fuzz arm hair feels soft and warm. I stop time in my head and just listen to Nancy's fleeting and finite breaths, and I think of her baby's cooing. Everything just stops for me. Everything just has to stop.

And then I leave the room in a daze of last breaths and people with callings and losses and the ones leaving. I leave the room full of good-byes and love and final rites and my aliveness at that very moment. I go downstairs and the blond girl is sitting on a plush purple couch, and baby Georgia is sleeping in her arms. She looks tired. I see her eyes, and they call to me. They are calling.

"Would you mind holding the baby for me for a minute? I just want to go upstairs and be with my sister for a bit," she says, "but I'm scared the baby will wake up if she's put in her crib. She likes to sleep against a person, with the feel of a heartbeat."

I put my arms out, open wide, and take the sleeping baby. I settle into the warm spot left for me on the couch and I cradle the slow-breathing baby, bringing her head up to my face and taking in the smell of flesh and powder and sleep. I watch Nancy's sister walk off, up toward Nancy's room, toward the end.

I survey the room. Because I am going to have to take something with me. Something of Nancy's. Because this is the end. Because this is my ritual. Because another one is about to die and I am here, a witness to this. I rock back and forth, in unison with the baby's deep, simple, certain breaths, trying to figure out what I will take.

CHECKMATE

L AST SUMMER I WENT TO VISIT my father in Italy. My girlfriend, Claudia, and I were getting married, and I wanted to ask my father, in person, to be my best man.

I knew Claudia was the woman I could be with. She was nicely plump, soft, with cornstalk-blond hair, and she spoke in this light and breathy voice that poured out of her mouth like warm bathwater, untouched. I met her through her younger brother Jamie, who was a member of the youth chess league that I'd been running for a few years. I love everything about chess: the order, the logic. I love how every piece has its role: the rook, who can move as far as he wants as long as he moves in a straight line, and the prestigious king, who can move in any direction he wants but only one space per turn. I love how even the lowly pawn, if he gets to the other side of the board, can become a queen.

Claudia wanted to wait until we were married to have sex. She was Christian, and strictly following a Christian walk. She'd let other things happen, but she didn't like to go down on me; sometimes she would do it if really persuaded. What happened between Claudia and me was what could happen until we were married. And what happened between Jamie and me a few weeks before I went to visit my father was not what should have happened. It was a moment of weakness, just weakness, and it was done and it was over and it just was. It just happened.

I was dropping Jamie off after an evening chess tournament. We beat the Bishop Shanahan High School team that night, finally. I was excited, pumped up. Jamie was quiet, unfazed. The funny thing about teenagers is that one year can make all the difference. In one year, Jamie had grown four inches taller and had become ten times quieter. Jamie had also gotten noticed by girls. I would watch from a distance as the girls on the chess team flirted with him, flipping their hair, talking real fast with their head turned down in that insecure and self-conscious way that girls do. When they did this, there was this grimace stuck on Jamie's face, but at the same time he flirted right back with them.

When we got to Jamie and Claudia's house, I went inside with him, so that I could leave Claudia a note. Claudia still lived at home, but she was out that night with her girlfriends shopping for bridesmaid dresses. Claudia's parents were in Barbados on a snorkeling trip, so the house was empty. Jamie and I walked in through the back door, into the large and airy kitchen, with its terra cotta floor tiles, making a person's walk across the floor known: squeaky if in sneakers, tap tap if in heels.

CHECKMATE

Jamie didn't even turn on the light. He went straight to the fridge, opened it, and a cut of light spread across the floor, showering across half of his face, his lean physique. He bent over slightly, leaning down to grab a soda. And there it was, his bent body, his light brown hair grown long in a harmless rebellion and pushed behind his ears, that tough-guy grimace on his face. In the light. And then I forgot everything I knew. In the middle of the light, I just moved forward to him. My hand reached out to his neck, pushing his hair back, and I was scared and I had to shit suddenly and I waited for him to jump up and call me an asshole and run or turn around and punch me right in the jaw, but instead, he leaned his neck back into my hand.

And the refrigerator door shut, and hands were moving all over the place and we were alone, in the kitchen, no light left. We were in the dark.

To get to my father's I flew into Rome and then caught a train south to the city of Naples, where he lives with his two brothers. I flew on Alitalia, a friendly airline where all the beautiful flight attendants treat you like you're the last man on earth, with their air of sexuality and their glistening lips, offering me wine every ten minutes. I kept saying, *No, thank you*, but they kept offering.

Naples is chaos. Sheer, unadulterated chaos. It is nothing like the calming images of Tuscany and Umbria and their colorful hill towns. Naples is oppressive, a jet-black backdrop, and the only splash of color is from the coastline it borders, the Golfo di Napoli. The Italians joke about Naples. During an argument or even playful banter, instead of telling a person to go to hell, they tell them to go to Naples.

My father left Naples when he was 22 years old to sail the seas. He became a crew member on the yacht of a wealthy family from Milan. He met my mother at port in New York a few years later; my mother had just turned 19. They married three weeks later, settled in Myrtle Beach, South Carolina, where my father found work chartering boats, and then they had me and then my sister, Dana, in quick succession. My mother left him two years after Dana was born and took us to Philadelphia, where my mother's sisters live. A family created and dispersed in such a flash. It was quick. As if it didn't even happen.

My father is a tall and impressive man, handsome and strapping. He has a wiry gray beard, wrinkled and sun-spotted skin from his time spent on a ship's deck crossing the Atlantic, Pacific, Caribbean, and Indian Oceans. His teeth are spaced far apart, yellow from a lifetime of tobacco and espresso. His English is still horrible despite all the years he lived in the States, but his accent is lyrical, almost like music.

For most of my life, my dad has been like a big elephant in the living room of our lives that everyone pretended wasn't there. As children, Dana and I would visit him in South Carolina once a year, but I never really knew him. His efforts were minimal. He never came to Philadelphia, and he would call us only on our birthday. I have only one memory that could explain why my mother left him, but this memory is cracked and yellow-gray, like an old sepia picture: My mother is in the kitchen of our house in Myrtle Beach, holding me, my sister, Dana, is in another room, probably in her playpen, screaming, and my father screaming too, and there was blood coming from somewhere on my mother's face, dripping onto my arm and she was holding me so tight, squeezing so hard, so hard I felt like I would suffocate.

My mother died years ago from breast cancer. All my life she never answered our questions about our father, which, going unanswered for so long, eventually stopped being asked. But then when my father moved back to Italy, around the time my mother was dying, he began to write me long letters. With a continent between us and my mother almost gone, my father began to emerge. Every week almost, I would receive a letter from him. In page after page of broken sentences, he told me about his childhood, his uncle's flaring gout and his grandfather's drunken rages. He told me about the stray dogs that would line up in the alley behind his house because his mother would give them scraps. He told me about his years on the world's oceans and all the islands he stopped at, like Jamaica and Providenciales and St. Lucia and St. Kitt. He told me how in Italy now, he spends his Sundays playing poker or chess with the old-timers like himself down by the water, how the salt air cures him of his troubles.

My father lives a few blocks from the train station. I walked from the station onto the crowded streets. I was immediately disoriented, overwhelmed. Families of three precariously perched on small scooters weaving in and out of the heavy traffic, loaded down with bags of groceries. The cars are tiny and, along with the scooters and motorcycles, loud and fumy, cram the narrow streets. The density and mayhem of traffic is like a moving wall, mere centimeters between cars pushing forward. But remarkably, if you just walk out into the road to cross the street, the cars will stop. Crossing the street is an eerie art, a leap of faith: You stand there on the curb, you wait until your gut tells you it feels right, and then you just walk into the street. You surrender, and everything stops.

My father lives on Corso Garibaldi, a street that cuts through the Piazza Garibaldi. I walked to his place on streets that were lined by vendors, espresso bars, restaurants, electronics shops. I found my father's place, tucked in like all city dwellings are: You can't see it at first, even though it is right in front of your face. He was living with his two brothers in a small apartment on 455 Garibaldi, right next to the Pensione Casanova, a small but clean *pensione* that the three of them own and run. There was a tall iron gate right on the sidewalk, facing the street, and passing through it brings you into a diamond-shaped courtyard where there is a tobacco shop, the entrance to the *pensione*, and my father and uncles' apartment. You can hear dogs barking and the chaos of the street, which is simmered down to background noise. The tobacco shop owner was outside sweeping away imaginary debris. The courtyard was clean relative to the rest of the city, whose tenement-like buildings in narrow streets remind you of old black-and-white pictures of New York City during the Great Depression.

I went to the front desk of the *pensione,* and a young man was standing there, writing something in the worn and tattered reservations book. His thick dark hair was slicked back and his skin was brown like packed clay. He took a cigarette from the pack of Peter Stuyvesants on the counter and lit it.

He looked up at me, with a slow and lazy gaze, "Ha bisogno di una camera per questa sera?" he said.

I stared at him, tired from the long flight and train ride. I knew he was asking me a question, but I couldn't understand him. I don't speak Italian.

"Ha bisogno di una camera per questa sera?" he repeated.

"Do you speak English?" I asked.

"A little," he said, squinting at me, ready to concentrate on what I had to say.

"My dad—Anthony Scardiglia—I'm looking for my dad."

His face perked up, recognizing his boss's name. "Prego. Prego," he said quickly, "Yes. Yes. You Nick? Yes?" he asked.

"Yes, I'm Nick," I said. He pointed to a set of double doors that led to a small porch. I put my bags down in the lobby, which was filled with old wicker furniture, and walked out into the thick and warm air. My father and his two brothers were sitting around a short and rectangular wooden table. My father and one uncle were playing chess. On the table was a scratched and well-worn chess table next to a full ashtray and a large carafe of wine. They were playing chess, and at that moment something in my father's life connected to mine, all in just a chessboard. We both know how to move the pieces.

My father and uncles all look alike, with ample mustaches. They were smoking furiously, my father contemplating his next move, all of them talking loudly and gesticulating with all the hands they had. They all turned to face me, wide grins spreading across their faces and suddenly I was surrounded by a flock of men, still holding their cigarettes, hugging me, slamming me on the back. I didn't know who was who because I was surrounded, by these men, my father, my uncles, all of these men, in a swirl of smoke and Italian.

The apartment that my father and two uncles live in next to Pensione Casanova barely holds the three of them comfortably. My father gave me a room in the *pensione,* which itself is also small, only 12 rooms. Pensione Casanova. Like the title of a bad romance novel or a place that cheating couples go to for an illicit rendezvous. Casanova, that promiscuous and unscrupulous of lovers.

The walls were thin in the hotel, as if your stay there was everyone's stay. All of your movements, words, and choices are filtered through the porous walls. I could hear the guests in the room next to me. I could hear them distinctly. It was two men. Two Australian men. Two young-sounding Australian men. They were talking about taking a day trip to Mount Vesuvius and Pompeii. After even ten hours in a foreign city, you become hyperaware of your own language, even if it's another accent, of your own voice, even in someone else's.

My father met Claudia, only once, a few months after we started dating. He made a trip back to the States and he was passing through Philadelphia to see me and Dana. I wanted everything to be perfect, because he was coming to see us. I made plans: I got tickets for us to see a special showing of *Touch of Evil,* an old Orson Welles movie from 1958 with Charlton Heston and Janet Leigh. My father had told me how much he liked Charlton Heston. And I made dinner reservations at Toscano's, a closet-size Italian restaurant. Claudia and Dana were going to join us for dinner. I wanted so badly to give my father an Italian meal. I wanted him to have his choice of fresh fish dishes, risotto made every half hour, pasta fagioli with pureed white beans and lots of al dente spaghetti.

The day before he arrived, I called Dana to remind her what time dinner reservations were at. She was crabby and miserable about our father's impending arrival, and considering backing out.

"Just why are you so happy about him visiting? And what is it with this bullshit *Ozzie and Harriet* Day Out with Dad crap?" she asked, unable to control herself.

"Why shouldn't I be happy about seeing him?" I asked, trying not to get sucked in by her anger.

"Maybe you haven't noticed, Nick, but he's been pretty much nonexistent our entire lives and then he just waltzes in town as if it is the most normal thing in the world," she said, her voice overflowing with years of disappointment.

"Listen, I feel like I'm finally getting to know him. What is so wrong with that?"

"Everything is wrong with it. He could have come to see us before this. He has only tried when we came to him, when it was convenient for him."

"Listen, Mom kept us from him, and told us nothing. Why are you blaming him for that?"

"Because he did nothing about it. Doesn't that bother you? Have you thought to ask him why he hasn't made much effort until now?"

"I've thought about it, but I don't know, Dana. I mean, I don't know how to ask him about these things."

"Well, I asked him. Unlike you, I don't sit around pretending everything's okay and not asking questions because I'm too frightened of the answers."

"Dana, I'm not frightened of anything," I said.

"Right, Nick. Sure thing. So that's why you plan this pic-ture-perfect day for his grand arrival, so you can feel like you're having this father-son moment, creating a memory, the whole kit-and-caboodle. You really want to get to know him, Nick? Then ask him a few questions about why he never came to visit us."

"Well, what did he say when you asked him that?"

"He said nothing, Nick. He changed the subject. He hung up on me one time when I kept at him with questions. He's like you, Nick—he prefers to be in the dark."

On my second day in Naples, my father and I spent the after-noon touring the city. He showed me the Royal Palace, the Cer-tosa di San Martino, and the dock where the boats leave every hour for the island of Capri. I found it easy to be among my fa-ther and uncles. They spoke so much Italian that I could just sit there and not have to say or do anything in particular. I could just be there, in their native and certain presence. They were allowed to be exactly who they wanted to be, and I cher-ished that. I wanted to be that: Myself. Native. At ease.

That evening my father and I walked over to Piazza Garibaldi. We took an outdoor table at a small restaurant. My fa-ther ordered a bottle of red wine and course after course of food.

A father and son who know each other well and have years of history and personal experiences—trips to the emergency room for stitches, baseball practice, getting yelled at for not tak-ing out the garbage—they can read each other's faces and expressions and body language. I wanted my dad to be my best man, to stand up for me now when I needed it most. In the letters he had been sending me, he wrote about how when he was a kid, his father left the house every morning at 2 AM to bake bread, how he saw his father only for an afternoon's moment when he'd come through the door in a cloud of flour and sweat, how the lines on his father's face were like an oak tree showing the years of life. My father knew his father's face, could read it all. I wanted my father to read my face, to see what I wanted, to know what I needed.

I drank a large glass of wine, and then another found its way to my hands, to my mouth, to my relief. I drank more wine, and ate all that was put in front of me: ensalada verde, penne arrabiata, rosemary chicken. I found myself with a full belly and a quiet calm of near drunkenness overcoming me and making it easy for me to see the two of us at table, the scene of my father and I sitting there, as something safe.

"Dad, you know I came all the way over here—to Naples— for a reason," I said.

"Yes. To see my Naples. To see where you are from, where your blood is from," he said, taking a big gulp of wine and lighting an unfiltered cigarette.

"I also came here to ask you something, too."

"Ask me," he said, grinning a satiated smile.

"Well, you know, Claudia and I are getting married at Christmas. We're having a wedding the day after Christmas."

"Yes. Yes. She is beautiful girl. Very beautiful. She will make good wife and mother."

"Yes, she will make a good wife and mother. I want you to come and be my best man in our wedding." I said.

"Come to the wedding? You want me to come to wedding in States, at Christmas?" he asked, slowly crouching down in his seat. "I see what I can do, you know, with hotel and all. Your uncles, they go La Spezia for week of Christmas. Every year. They do this. Who will watch hotel? I don't know. We see. I see."

"But I don't want you to just come, I want you to be my best man. Don't you see?" I asked.

"Dad, don't you see?" I repeated.

"We see. We see," he said.

Later that night, I sat on my bed in Room 8, my mouth dry from all the wine, a headache approaching. I hated my sister Dana at that very moment for being right.

Claudia wanted Jamie to be the best man anyway. I knew this. Jamie was the reason that Claudia and I met; she had said that a few times, right after I put the engagement ring on her finger. "If it wasn't for Jamie . . ." she'd say, twirling the ring, swaying her head from side to side with the combination of naiveté and the conviction that all is secure and right just because a diamond was on her left hand. When I got back from Italy, there would be no sound or rational reason that I could give to Claudia why Jamie shouldn't be my best man.

I was numb and everything was still. I watched television. An episode of *Knight Rider* was on, dubbed in Italian. I couldn't understand a word that was being said and yet miraculously, I could follow the plot. Then, right there, my bed started to shake from the wall, from the bed against the wall in the room next to me. I could hear the people in the next room, the Australian guys, grunting and occasionally moaning. The violence of their movements and pushing and shoving. My attention went to them and I was hard and my hand went down and I couldn't help myself. After a while, things quieted down, my bed came to a standstill.

I felt gritty, dirty, and agitated, so I went to take a shower. There were no bathrooms in the rooms; instead, there was one bathroom at the end of the hall. I was walking to the bathroom, and one of the guys from the next room stepped out into the hallway, heading for the bathroom also. He was only wearing a towel. His face was red and his chest damp—the hairs clinging around his navel and right under his arms. I stared at him, trying to figure out how to turn my attention away, how to stop being hard, how to get back to where I came from

"You can go first," I stammered, "because I'm going to take a shower, I might be a while."

"Thanks, mate," he said. "Just need to take a whiz."

He walked past me quickly, heading off to the bathroom. He had left the door to their room open a bit, and I wondered about his partner in there. I waited in the hall. The Australian guy was out of the bathroom quickly.

"Thanks again," he said, walking by with a large grin.

I took my shower. But I was still bothered and sweating. I dressed and decided to go somewhere and get a drink. To get fresh air. To get something. I headed back to the bathroom—I forgot why halfway down the hall—maybe to shave or brush my teeth or something. For something. Coming into the hallway again was the Australian guy I had just seen.

"We meet again," he said, grinning. He was holding a valet case.

I smiled.

"But this time I'll wait. You go first," he said.

"Thanks."

"Alone are ya?" he asked.

"Excuse me?" I asked, not sure what he meant.

"You alone? Me and my mate Larry are going to go get a drink somewhere. Wanna join us?"

"I don't drink," I said, lying out of a sudden and irrational fear. But then I immediately regretted this lie and wanted to badly get out of it. I wanted out of this lie.

"Well, you're welcome to come out with us anyway. My name's David. Just come by. We're leaving in about 15 minutes. Haven't come across many Americans here. We love Americans. So join us if you'd like."

"Thanks," I said.

"Right-o," he said, "or I suppose I should say *Prego*," he chuckled.

He went into his room. I shaved quickly, but carefully, not wanting to cut myself. And then I went next door. I knocked. David opened the door and welcomed me in. He knew it. David knew I would come.

The next morning I was tired and sore. I was out too late, too long. I was ready to go home. I wanted now to put Naples behind me. There would be no best man when I left this city.

My father was working all day at the front desk of the *pensione,* so I went by myself to the Museo Nazionale, a dusty museum full of relics from Pompeii and Greek and Roman sculptures. School kids surrounded me, their echoes loud in the wide halls. Larger-than-life statues of perfectly sculpted naked men in marble filled the halls. There were no electronic monitoring systems, no ropes holding you back. You could touch the statues and take pictures. Crowds of dark little Italian boys surrounded a statue of a Roman god with a hairless chest. The boys were laughing, bending down to touch the statue's mammoth feet. Everyone was welcome to add to the deterioration.

After the museum I walked to the crèche district, a cluster of allcylike streets with shop after shop that sells crèche figures: painstakingly hand-painted members of the Nativity scene. Thousands of Josephs, Marys, baby Jesuses, the Three Wise Men, lambs and mules and cows. Some of the clay figures looked like baby Jesus but were actually little angels. Two thousand lire, just $1.50, for a baby Jesus or an angel with wings.

I bought some crèche figures for Claudia. I could give her the Nativity scene as a Christmas gift. It was something that I know she would love. At another store I found shelves stacked with chili pepper ornaments; the chili pepper is a sign of good luck in Italy. Some of the ornaments were like a male version of the mermaid: half pepper, half man. I bought Claudia five pepper ornaments, to bring her lots of luck. Later, when I was back at home and wrapping the crèche figures and the pepper ornaments, I would discover that many of them didn't survive the trip. The jostling of the bags and packages were too much. The angels took the worst hit: the arms of one were broken and the wings of the other ones were cracked.

Catholicism is epitomized in Naples. Churches and cathedrals and duomos are everywhere. If you want God or need God or are looking for any sign of God, He can be found in Naples. Dug into the walls of buildings are small shrines to Mary and to countless saints. None of these shrines are vandalized or desecrated despite the poverty and the petty crime that proliferates. Jesus and Mary, at least in Naples, are truly sacred.

I came across a shrine to Saint Francesco Di Paolo. It was at eye level, in the wall of a building on a coal-black street. The blessed Saint's picture was fading from age, and he had long gray hair; there were candles around his picture in which he stood there with open arms, welcoming everyone, all of us. I walked into the Saint Francesco Di Paolo church that was around the corner. An early afternoon Mass was letting out and old Italian women, short women wearing peasant dresses, shuffled past me. A few old men followed. In the pews a few women remained, on their knees, clutching their crucifixes with their heads bowed and their lips muttering in prayer.

I saw a confession box at the back of the church. A small white sign was hanging near the box: *Aperto 13:00 to 14:00.* I knew that *aperto* meant "open."

Confession was *aperto.* Open.

I walked into the confession box. I didn't have to. But there it was. The box. For confession. And I wanted to leave it all in Naples. I wanted to leave everything that I brought, that I asked for, that I didn't get, and that I found. I pulled the confession box door shut.

I even knew the opening line, which I delivered on my knees, "Bless me, Father, for I have sinned."

"Mi dispiace figliolo, non parlo inglese," he replied.

I couldn't understand him. I could see the shadow of the priest through the wooden mesh board of the confession box. The green curtain of the confession box closed me off to the rest of the church, to the outside world, to the Australian guys and my father and Jamie and Claudia. It was just me and the priest in this small wooden box, and I could tell him everything. I could just leave all of it here: my lined up pawns and stricken knights and leveled rooks. But I couldn't understand what the priest was saying. I started to sweat a bit, and decided to try again.

DEEP DOWN
TO THE BOTTOM OF THIS

NIGEL, HIS COLLEAGUE DR. LOUISA STEELE, my coworker Justine, and I were having dinner together at the Intercontinental Hotel in downtown Chicago. It was the second evening of the Annual Meeting of the Crustacean Society. For one week, biology professors from every imaginable crevice of academia came out of their dusty offices with poor lighting to discuss the latest migratory and demographic happenings of crabs and shrimp and lobsters and all those strange, prehistoric-looking pinkish-encrusted creatures that live in oceans, seas, and lakes.

Nigel was presenting a paper that year on Lake Michigan's declining numbers of diporeia, a tiny shrimplike crustacean. The decreasing number of this important link in the food chain was wreaking havoc for other fish. According to Nigel's paper,

all of this was the fault of the zebra mussel. Although technically Nigel was retired, he held an adjunct title in the Biology
Department at the University of Pennsylvania. He and Dr.
Louisa Steele had written a textbook that was the gold standard
for almost every biology major in every university across the
country. And that is why Justine and I were there: We were
from the publisher of this gold mine of a book. Justine was the
marketing representative; she was a short waify girl with one of
those crackly voices that sounds sexy if you are a guy and
highly annoying if you are one of her female coworkers. She
was there to stroke egos and show them leaflets, mailing initia-
tives, bind-in cards, and other promotional items that would be
used to generate more sales for the upcoming edition of their
book. I was there because I was the production representative—the techy. I was there to explain to Nigel and Dr. Steele
how I was going to get their printed book into every imaginable
electronic format—from CD-ROM to DVD to the Internet to
downloading it to a PDA, to even one day using it on those
minicomputers you hook around your head.

I had tried to warm these two crusty professors up to me,
hoping that the fact that I lived in the same city—Philadelphia—would help. But they were not interested in my spiel.
They were biologists with a fixation on crustaceans. It was as if
their livelihood kept them in the past, as if they were born old
and hard-shelled. As an electronic publishing techy, I had to
look forward, future bound, upward, brightward. So they
looked at me, baffled, as I rattled off a slew of abbreviations—
HTML, SGML, ASP, XML—that I knew could be outdated in
just a few years, maybe months, as the pace of technology
warp-speeded us to the next abbreviation. Nigel and Dr. Steele

were perennial academics who were born during World War II; the only abbreviation they probably cared about was SNAFU.

"That just means that something got fucked up, right?" I said to Nigel, one year after the crustacean meeting. I was in Nigel's bed, picking one of his gray hairs out of my mouth. We had just made love. He had claimed that his leg cramping up during lovemaking was merely a snafu. I knew better; his leg always cramped up when we made love and he always complained about it, but he always forgot about having complained about it.

"I think you need to look the word up, my dear. *Fucked up* is a bit base, don't you think, for defining an important military acronym?"

After Nigel was asleep I looked up SNAFU. And Webster's told the tale of his dry British sense of humor.

SNAFU—Situation normal all fucked up.

I did not know that week when I met Nigel—and his wife, Ulita—that he would become my lover, let alone my husband. When I was 13 years old, my friend Theresa Sellman's mom told me that sometimes you meet the man you are going to marry long before you know you even like him, let alone that you will marry him. I felt nothing near like, nor love nor hate, when I first met Nigel that night at the Intercontinental Hotel. I didn't even feel indifferent. What I felt was surprised. It was because of dinner: I really wanted to order the prawn special that evening, but I figured it would be a professional blasphemy to order anything in a shell from under the sea, so I played it safe and got a pork chop stuffed with corn and bacon, dressed with port-braised collards. It shocked me to watch as Dr. Steele order the prawn special and then Nigel order grilled shrimp in a coconut curry. It was like watching a mother eat its young.

I never outright intended to marry a man 30 years older than me. It wasn't what I planned consciously, knowingly. Loving older men was because of habit, because of histories both good and bad—because of an evolution that took seed at 15 and then surfaced when I was 17 years old and it just never ended, this habit.

Evan Cooksley was the first older man I fell in love with. Like the first kiss, the first cigarette, the first hangover. I was 17 and he was 31. Evan was an underwriter for a small insurance firm where I worked after school every Tuesday, Thursday, and Friday. The company was in an old Victorian home converted into offices. It was rumored that the house was haunted by the wife of the original owner; within a few weeks of moving in, the wife had died of consumption. (I wanted to ask Evan what consumption was when he was telling me the story, but I didn't want him to think I was stupid—I was so consumed by him.) After the wife died, the owner had a life-size stained-glass window made of her image—she was in an angelic flowing gown of blue, with her long brown tresses rolling down and around her shoulders. The giant window was near the staircase. I used to stare at the stained-glass window as I sat in the front room, answering phones, transferring calls to all the underwriters on the second floor: Mike, Nick, Tony, Chuck, and of course, Evan. Evan, who had a beard and was tall and who made me fumble and fluster and not know what to say. Evan, whose father and brother were New York City police officers.

I wanted something from Evan, the solidness of his age or at least what seemed solid to me then. I wanted the crow's feet just starting around his eyes. I wanted his knowing. At the time I wanted Evan, I had a boyfriend named Doug whom I loved and who loved me and whose body satisfied me. I had love already, and yet I wanted Evan. I got my best friend, Lydia, to come pick me up after work one day just so she could see Evan.

"Gross. He's like old," she said to me after she briefly met Evan and we got in her car, a loud Mazda Z28 that she called her father's midlife crisis car.

"He's only 31. That's not old," I said.

"That's totally old," she replied.

"His brother just died a few months ago. Brain cancer."

"And he's got a beard too. Even grosser," she said, not even hearing the cancer part.

Evan's first day back at the office after his brother's funeral was odd to me. I sorted mail and delivered it to the inboxes of each underwriter on the second floor. In the best of circumstances, I felt nervous, sweaty, and elated delivering the mail to Evan's office. Doing it the first day Evan was back after his brother's death was excruciating. I did not know what to say. The risk of it: Saying nothing. Saying something and having that something be the most wrong thing in the world to say. Our lives are filled with awkwardness of so many levels, and seeing a person for the first time after someone they loved has died feels like the most awkward. Because what I was thinking was blunt: *Your brother is dead. Gone. And I do not know what to say to you. Help me say something to you. I want to say some-*

thing to you. Help me. I want to touch your wrist and feel your neck and your brother is dead and I am sweating.

And I said something. Because when I walked into Evan's office, he did not try to hide his pain or anguish or anything from me and in doing that, I tripped toward my first moment of grace and said what I had to say: "I'm sorry about your brother."

He looked up at me, his beard looking even softer to me, and he said, "Thanks."

And then three months later, my father was dead from a heart attack that no man could ever survive and Evan sits me in his office and this time he talked and I couldn't say anything. He just talked and talked, words spilling out, tears in his eyes, and all that his brother was and could be was handed over to me, his grief set free to some 17-year-old filing clerk who madly wanted to unbutton his shirt, touch his beard, put her hand somewhere anywhere on his body. I did not hear him in so many ways, I felt not his pain over his brother and his brother's unfair death. I felt nothing like that. I could not talk about my father, because it still made no sense. But I could make sense of one thing: being in his office with the door closed and what we had in common—dead family. It was Evan, a love that was untouched. Tears over dead family in an office. All of it never understood. Fucked up. A risk never taken.

The love affair with Nigel began with a brooch. An oval-shaped brooch of gold that was set with a smooth amber stone. Nigel's wife, Ulita, and her brooch.

I was supposed to meet Nigel and Dr. Steele for breakfast to continue our conversation from the previous evening. We needed to finalize decisions about the Internet interface for their chapter on the barnacle. But plans changed: Nigel and Dr. Steele had already eaten and were much more interested in going over to the convention center to see the new display of scuba gear at one of the stands of a sponsoring aquatic equipment company. *Scuba*—self-contained underwater breathing apparatus—was the only other acronym a crustacean lover seemed to care about.

Ulita called me that morning in my hotel room to let me know that Nigel and Dr. Steele would not be meeting me for breakfast. Before I could say *Thank you,* she told me that she would be delighted to take their place. *Nigel told me what a nice young lady you are,* she said.

And even though I just wanted to catch an extra hour of sleep, I knew I could not say no. For a lot of reasons. Because it was rude. And because I knew that Ulita was dying. She was edging toward the end of her battle with lung cancer. Justine had told me. Her liver was already partly infested with extremely diligent cancer cells. Her bones were cracking, ready to break. And yet she came with Nigel to this meeting, came to meet me for breakfast, forging forward dying as old people with cancer do.

Ulita and I were seated in the same dining room as I had been with her husband the night before. Ulita was a tall, thin woman with porcelain skin, fluttery blue eyes, and long fingers. I did not know if she was thin because she was dying, or if she had always been a thin woman. After Nigel and I were together, he told me she had always been thin, which made her dying all the more unreal to him, as if she wasn't dying but just getting ready to leave him.

"I love your brooch," I said to Ulita, looking for conversation, not yet relaxed with her fleeting presence. "It looks like a family heirloom or something."

"The brooch was my mother's. When she left Russia, my grandmother pinned it to the inside of her jacket," Ulita said.

And even though I knew so little about history, about what happened in the time of Lenin or Stalin or either of the world wars, I did know this: You didn't just leave Russia. It was never just a come-and-go place. You were taken out of Russia or forced or smuggled out; you fled or escaped. You didn't just leave.

"It's beautiful. I've always wished I had really old family heirloom stuff like that. My grandparents all died before I was born, so I have so little in stories or even possessions. I wish I had some—it's history."

"Surely you have *some*?" she asked me, pushing her untouched eggs around the plate.

"Well, I have this one picture that must be from the mid-1800s. My mother gave it to me. She can't remember who it is, but we know it is someone from her side of the family. The resemblance is uncanny. It's a wedding picture, but just of the bride. She's wearing a wedding dress and holding a bouquet of flowers, but it's funny because she isn't smiling."

"Well, marriage—and history for that matter—isn't always something to smile about," Ulita said.

"Here," she continued, "I want you to have this." She reached under her olive-green cashmere sweater and began to unclasp the brooch. Her hands shook a bit.

"No. I can't take that," I said, embarrassed and nervous.

"But of course you can."

"Absolutely not, Ulita," I said, becoming more embarrassed. "Surely you want to give that to your children or your grandchildren."

"I have no grandchildren, and my daughter does not like jewelry. She has never even noticed this brooch and I have been wearing it forever. And I have so many other things that are being left for her."

"But you don't know me."

"But you know Nigel. And maybe you will know Nigel more."

"Excuse me?"

"I will die soon. Nigel will need to reach out to a woman. And you are one of the only smart women he has met in years. He told me so."

The conversation was beginning to scare me.

"But Dr. Steele is a smart woman. She's brilliant. And she's sort of good-looking, too," I stammered out, not knowing what I was talking about, grasping for straws. I did know the good-looking part was a blatant lie. Crustacean women were actually pretty ugly. They failed to tend to themselves: They needed a little hair dye, a shave under the pits, a plucking of the brows. Some lipstick wouldn't kill these women.

"Actually Dr. Steele is not brilliant. She just knows a lot about lobsters and crayfish. But she doesn't believe in God."

"I'm afraid I'm still not following you," I said, scanning back and forth across the room, hunkering down, suddenly concerned that someone would actually hear us.

"I'm talking about God. These crustacean women don't believe in God," she said.

I knew what Ulita was talking about. I had met with doctors Trotto and Tredynnick on the first day of the Crustacean Society meeting. The two women were writing a book for our company on experimental biology. They were telling me about a heated argument they had with some fundamentalist Christians who were outside the convention center to protest the forward movement of cloning among the biology discipline. The PETA people were outside protesting, too, but they didn't come to fight human cloning. They were more interested in screaming lobsters, whose nerve endings had rights far superior to that of research in the biological sciences. And somehow during this discussion outside the convention center, the people from PETA had managed to join forces with the fundamentalists, and I had to hold back my laughter. Doctors Trotto and Tredynnick saw no humor—they only saw black and white.

"Just who do these people think they are?" Dr. Tredynnick said. "Their whole creationism spiel is getting into the minds of young people and before you know it Darwin will be called a quack and the people who will be changing my diapers in my old age will think the earth is flat. This is nuts. Just nuts."

"Nigel believes in God," I said, more to myself than to Ulita.

"Well of course he does, Katherine. How could he not? Science. God. They can be in the same room together. I think that's half the reason he married me. I was a smart-talking, sexy, long-legged, God-fearing woman."

"But how do you even know I believe in God?" I asked.

Ulita didn't answer me. She just smiled and handed over the brooch. She looked young to me suddenly, as if something in her life suddenly shifted, got put in place. She looked like a woman whose life was making sense. She knew her husband. He was a man who would always have a wife. Some men are just like that. They are halves. They need a wife even if she is incompetent or overweight or too young or has bad teeth. They are not whole without the counterpart, the solidity of a gold ring on the third finger of their left hand. These men don't even know it, that they must be married, which is why they marry women who know it.

"Let's go have a sneaky," she said to me suddenly, her head lifting straight up, victorious.

"What's that?" I asked.

"A cigarette. Nigel's mother always called them that because she would sneak off to the porch after dinner to have one. And I'm dying for one," she said, grinning ear to ear at her own pun.

"I don't smoke," I said, leaving out the very important last word of my sentence: *anymore.*

"Did you ever?"

"Well, yeah, but I quit years ago," feeling hypnotized by this emaciated woman.

"Then you still miss them?" she asked, her logic unrefutable, reeling me in. How can one not miss them? The allure, the mouth, the inward and outward breaths, the danger and the risk.

I paid the check and we went outside. I held her up as we walked slowly through the gold-ceilinged lobby where people were arriving in cabs and departing with stuffed suitcases, where the world was moving and everything was comfortable. I held tight to her frail arm, through the revolving door and then we were outside the Intercontinental Hotel, standing on Michigan Avenue—the Magnificent Mile. Her hands trembled and fumbled for her cigarettes that she finally found buried deep in her red patent leather purse. I took the pack from her, put two in my mouth and tried to light them, the wind gusting at me, my hands cupping them. Ulita was leaned up against the wall of the hotel for support. I kept trying and finally lit both and I took the smoke in and it had been three years and my lungs hurt, taking it in, her brilliance, her dying brilliance, the smoke, the air.

Another reason I chose to marry a man entirely too old for me was because I needed to be able to unload my secrets.

By the time I reached my mid-thirties, my family had cornered the market on secrets. I was polluted and poisoned with them. I was lethargic from them. I was verbally threatened by siblings to keep them, silenced by others who knew I may reveal them. All those secrets: someone taking way too much Valium, someone taking even more Vicodin, some time on the psych ward, outrageous inconceivable debt, abortions, infidelity, electroshock therapy before it was vogue. Shhhhhhhhhhhh.

I needed a man who would listen to my secrets and I was repeatedly learning that men in their thirties don't want that much information. (Ryan shut down. Kenneth walked out.) Men in their sixties have already lived. They have had affairs and Valium. They have smelled the rot of our lives, siphoned through shattered marriages and car crashes, dead parents, illness, tooth extraction, lying, pretending, and all the dark moments that we cannot, will not, no no never avoid. I could unburden myself to an old man, a solid man, an experienced man, a man who had been through years and wars and difficulty, who had seen an ample share of death and pain and sadness.

I could tell only a much older man the one secret that was solely mine and that nobody knew and that I couldn't share to anyone: how when I was 15 years old and spending the weekend with my godparents, the man who was my godfather would have a sleight of hand. There, lying on the couch with me watching cable (my godmother, who I called Aunt Sissy, was upstairs, asleep, tired with the fatigue that three children render), that he and I lay there, our bodies opposite each other, he said to me, my feet at his hands, his at mine, "Let's rub each other's feet."

And I didn't want to, but we did, and there and then I knew forever my world had changed, that nothing was what I thought it was, that with the first touch of his thick fingers on the sole of my feet (penetrating my soul it seemed), that everything had changed. And then he switched his position, turned and laid down in my direction, spooning me and I pretended immediately—I was a quick study—that nothing had changed and then his hand was there, sliding up from my hip, up my waist, under my breast, and then the moment froze: A godmother upstairs asleep. Cable television. My godfather's hand. A father. No God.

I needed an older man who was going to listen to this bundle of shame. I knew I could never marry a man I couldn't tell this to, that I could never give my whole body and my legs and arms and breasts and mouth eternally, my soul and my insides forever, that I couldn't give it to a man unless I could tell him how someone had already unjustly tried to lay claim to it. (I was no saint. I was no virgin. I did not have sexual hang-ups. I wrapped my body around other men's bodies and loved and needed, but I would never marry a man whom I could not tell of this trespassing.) It was a risk either way you cut it: Keeping the secrets and suffocating. Letting them out to breathe, to take up space, to land where they will land, to be in ears and brains and the hearts of others.

At the time I met Nigel, I ached. It was like every nerve on the front of my body—over my heart, my belly, my breasts, my knees—was cross-sectioned during the night in a dream or under cover of an anesthetic in the air. I needed so much to be held. I was scared of this. I couldn't even tell anyone, how much I wanted to be held. I suppose I could have found a man, some man, any man, to hold me, to lie flat on top of me and cure the ache and find the nerves and get this cross section back to the rest of my body, but I was scared to just take any man. Because I was teeming with secrets, desperate for love, unable to take the risk without knowing the risk was worth taking. And with Nigel I knew what was on the table: an old man with a dying wife; the wife will die; the old man will die before you. I wish I could say it was a difficult decision. I wish I could say I had guilt and felt bad and thought I was using Nigel. But I could face the facts: that I was lonely, that Nigel needed a wife, that I needed to unburden my secrets, that I needed a man older than me anyway because it was all I knew and you have to face these things, you have to accept what you know, you have to face not loving someone. You have to risk growing to love them.

⌐⅍⌐

Ulita and I were on the second floor of the Art Institute of Chicago. After breakfast and sneakies, Ulita convinced me to skip my duties for the day—manning our company booth with a bunch of sales reps—and join her for a few hours at the Art Institute.

I had never been to the Art Institute, and I was surprised at how much recognizable art filled the hallways. I felt like I was in a room full of fake pictures. At every corner was a painting I recognized, but I could not pinpoint when I had seen it for the first time (an art history lesson in seventh grade? a coffee table book of famous paintings?). All the recognition was coming from an unknown place in my mind, a buried secret resurfacing: Georges Seurat's *A Sunday on la Grande Jatte,* with all the people made up of little dots and the women with bustles and corsets, holding umbrellas on the grass next to the water; Edward Hopper's *Nighthawks,* with the dark backdrop of greens and the only diner patron who has bright color is the red-haired woman in the fuchsia shirt who looks at her nails while the man in his white uniform and cap behind the counter leans over; and Andy Warhol's 15-foot silk screen *Mao.*

I pushed Ulita through the museum in a wheelchair. She was too weak to walk for a few hours, and suddenly we were staring at the grim, stone faces of Grant Wood's *American Gothic*—the farmer holding a pitchfork, standing there with his spinster daughter. Until that moment when I read the placard next to the painting, I had always assumed the woman in the picture was his wife, not his daughter.

"Don't you think the risk of not having faith is just too high?" Ulita asked me.

I barely heard her question. I was staring at the pitchfork the father was holding. How close they stood to each other. The tragedy and harshness and risks they must have faced.

"Don't you think, Katherine, that the risk of not having faith is just too high?" she repeated, tugging at my arm, looking up at me from the confines of the wheelchair.

"Faith in what?" I asked.

"All of it. Love. God. Science. Art."

"I couldn't agree with you more," I said. "But I have doubts. Big ones. Solid faith in just about anything is sort of tough these days."

"But Doubt is the father of Faith," Ulita said to me, almost excited, smiling, still holding onto my arm.

⌒⁘⌒

Two months after Ulita died, Nigel came to my apartment to ask for the brooch back.

"Nigel, is that you?" I spoke into my apartment intercom.

I recognized Nigel's voice, the rasp, the way age crept through the windpipes.

"Yes, Katherine, it's me. May I come up?"

"Of course," I said, and I pressed the release button and met him at the elevator.

I welcomed him into my apartment, which is always clean. It is the only place I can find control these days. I am too sensible to find control in this world through eating disorders or obsessive exercising; I also, quite frankly, lack the vanity. I quite like my belly, the way it hangs over my belt line a bit. I think of it as Rubenesque, sexy. My breasts have become a bit pendulous, and that too, I become more comfortable with as 35 approaches. But I still need control, a little bit, somewhere.

I got Nigel comfortably seated on my couch and began to make a pot of tea.

"Well, Katherine, I'm afraid I have something I need to ask you. I feel quite sheepish, and I don't know where to begin."

My back was facing Nigel, so he couldn't see me shake and my hands indeed began to shake because honestly I thought he was going to propose right then, despite our not having had a date nor anything Ulita said to me during our time in Chicago having really surfaced. It still lay in sediment, deep down, covered over by what is rational and normal and suburban and television-like. Deep down it rested, in its quiet tomb, no risk.

It was silent in my apartment for what seemed like minutes. You could hear the clink of my tea cups, the opening of my refrigerator, pouring milk into a creamer, finding the sugar, the sounds of making something, creating a small and warm and basic comfort for a British man whose wife was dead.

"It's the brooch," Nigel finally said.

"The brooch?"

"Yes, the one Ulita gave to you."

"How did you know she gave it to me?" I asked.

"Well, she told me of course—that she gave it to you."

"Of course," I said, quickly recovering, embarrassed by my insensitivity, "I mean, of course she told you. Oh, gosh, I suppose you want it back. Oh Nigel, I'm so sorry. I mean, I—" and I stopped myself there because it was another discovery about how Ulita and Nigel told each other everything. There were no secrets.

"She really did want you to have it," he said. "The only reason I have to ask for it back is because of our daughter Anna.

Nigel looked older than ever. His hands trembled as he picked up his cup of tea, his lips quivering a bit as he sipped. He looked sad, burdened, tired.

"Of course, Nigel. You don't have to explain. Let me get it for you," I said.

"You see you need to understand what this brooch really means," he said to me.

"Nigel, you don't have to explain," I said emphatically, feeling tears welling up in my eyes. I wanted the brooch, a piece of old old history that I did not know. But it was a history that was not my own and so I wanted it.

"Do you know how Ulita came to this country?"

"No," I said, "I don't."

"Ulita's mother, whose name was Zerka, was from the USSR. She lived in the city of Zhdanov, which was on the Sea of Azov, a tiny inlet of the Black Sea. After the Battle of Stalingrad, Zerka, who was only 19 years old, was dragged from her home by German soldiers. The Germans had lost the Battle of Stalingrad, but they were still strong. So while withdrawing, they stopped into all the homes at Zhdanov and dragged the young people out. Zerka's mother, knowing she'd never see her daughter again, quickly pinned the brooch on the inside of Zerka's sweater, giving Zerka what small piece of her history and world and life on the Black Sea she could. Zerka and hundreds of other young people were put on trains to go work in German factories. Zerka screamed as she was taken out of her parents' house."

Nigel took a sip of his tea and a deep breath, as if reliving Ulita's mother's history was reliving his own.

"Ironically enough," Nigel continued, "the train broke down in the middle of nowhere. It was there, among this crowd, that Zerka met a man named Nicholas. They were far from home, close to nowhere, and they knew they could not go home because once you were captured by the Germans, the Soviets really only wanted you back dead. So they just walked. That was all they could do. They walked. Eventually, after dodging both German soldiers and Allied bombings, Zerka and Nicholas ended up in Stuttgart, which wound up in the American sector. The Allies sorted everyone out and put the Eastern European refugees in displaced persons camps by nationality. That's where Zerka and Nicholas called themselves husband and wife and it is where they had a child named Ulita, in a Ukranian DP camp a few months after the war ended."

I was silenced.

"Anna doesn't know you have the brooch. But I think she should have it. It's history."

I started to cry. Because the brooch was never supposed to be mine. It wasn't meant for me. It wasn't supposed to get so far through all of this, from near the Black Sea through a sea of risk and then be mine forever. It wasn't meant to be mine—not the brooch.

With Nigel gone now, my risks are minimized. I'm almost out of risks altogether: I am comfortable, and I have my health. I am 40 years old.

The way I see it, I can wind up being like my Aunt Mimi, if I work at it a little, get myself out on a date or two. My Aunt Mimi had no children and two husbands, both of them Ph.D.'s; both of them died on her. She also had a house in Ocean City, New Jersey.

All I need now is a second husband who is also a doctor and a house by the Jersey Shore. Hurricanes still hit the Jersey Shore, but it has been decades since real destruction has come out of a wicked swirling storm. I remember as a child, when Aunt Mimi was with her second doctor, living there at the Shore, Hurricane Bertha came roaring in and knocked homes down and roofs off, lifting things far and away. Aunt Mimi called my mother to report that her washing machine had traveled seven blocks and was discovered at the corner of 5th Street and Ocean Boulevard.

"How did you know it was yours, Mimi?" my mother asked. I was ten years old and sitting at the kitchen table, and my mother was smoking a cigarette and talking on a bright yellow telephone with a cord that curled tight like a hair on Shirley Temple's head.

"Because it still had my underwear in it," she said, laughing so loud I could hear her.

I always knew it would be impossible for Nigel to outlive me. Impossible for me to have him the rest of my life. Nigel and I were married for five years; having him for only five years was not shocking. What was shocking was for him to die of something other than disease: Not cancer or a stroke or a cardiovascular event. No anemias or multiple myeloma or pulmonary embolisms or brain aneurysms. My husband died in a scuba diving accident. The crusty crustacean whom I grew to love was never found, his body never recovered. It was probably a problem with the control device or the oxygen tanks or something but he never surfaced, his body is somewhere deep down there, somewhere in the sea.

Once I took him as my husband, I knew I had entered an hourglass and I knew two things would come: relief and death. I wanted relief, and I long ago accepted that all of us are guaranteed at least one death.

I knew what was possible and impossible walking in. This is all because of so many things: histories, German soldiers and brooches, a slide of a godparent's hand, a secret I had to keep, the need to marry a man too old for me just so I could unload this secret and burden and have a shot at a marriage that was secret free, a dying woman whose husband needed a living one.

I have never wanted the possible in what seems impossible: a life forever stretched by stem cells or respirators or legal documents or cryogenics; a child of mine manufactured and carefully selected from my vast pool of DNA in a petri dish, taking the prettiest and bestest sliver—instead of melding my body with another and coming and waiting and seeing what happens; a pig's kidneys to replace my rotting ones; a house wired so intricately that I never need to turn on another switch or press another button or open another refrigerator door or turn on another heater or stove top—so that with this house all I have to do is talk, my voice recognized by my wired house, my voice talking back to me or to anyone whose footsteps it does not recognize.

BAD ASS BOB,
A MUG SHOT MUG, A MAN

G EORGE ASKED HIS ROOMMATE, Howard, where Daphne had been over the weekend. The two of them were on the patio of their first-floor apartment. I was above them, on the balcony of me and my wife Janice's apartment.

"It's over," Howard said.

"Oh yeah?" George said, sounding a bit perplexed, as if this was news to him too.

"Yeah. You know," Howard said.

There was a pause, a pause that lasted four inhales of the Marlboro Ultra Light cigarette I was smoking. I've gone from Marlboro Regular (red pack) to Marlboro Light (tan pack) to Marlboro Ultra Light (silver pack). I was silent on the balcony, smoking silver-pack cigarettes—silver so I can cut back, so maybe I can quit altogether, so maybe Janice can have some hope that my wrist will stop hurting, that things will change.

"I sent her an e-mail," Howard said to George, their voices carrying up and away with my cigarette smoke.

"You two are gonna keep in touch, then?"

"No. I mean that's how I ended it," Howard said. "I told her it isn't working out—I told her in an e-mail."

"Christ," George said, with a heavy but forgiving breath.

"Christ is right," Howard said, sounding relieved to get it off his chest.

I exhaled. The burn in my wrist spread out, traveling to the tips of my fingers.

The first time I saw Howard's girlfriend, Daphne, I was outside walking me and Janice's cat, Boots. I've heard Howard and George laugh under their breath while I'm walking Boots past their window. I know what they think, seeing me, a 45-year-old man, old enough to be their father, walking a cat. I know what it's like to be in your twenties. I know what they think: *pansy ass.* Once when I was walking Boots I heard one of them mutter under his breath—I could swear it was Howard—I could hear him joking, "Hey, here comes bad ass Bob."

Daphne had wide sexy hips and long brown hair with blond streaks in the front. That first time I saw her, she was hanging her head down low in that sheepish way when you first are really falling for someone and you are scared for anyone to know how much you feel. She was holding Howard's hand. Later I would notice that she had a big nose; it wasn't ugly-big, just big. She had a great mouth, full and sort of open, as if you could put your finger in it. She was hot. Unless they are really fat, almost all women have something about them that is hot. Even if they have a saggy ass or no tits or thin lips, there is something you can find in almost any woman that is hot. Otherwise they wouldn't be women.

"Something was missing with her," Howard continued. "I can't quite pinpoint it. But something was just missing."

You bet something was missing, I thought. To not face the girl, to not say *It's over* no matter the surprise and embarrassment and the stammering and the stuttering and that awful push you have to make to say it to their face. You bet something was missing, I thought: Your balls. Your motherfucking balls.

I'm a welder and I can't work because of the pain in my wrist. I've been on disability for 11 months—11 months, two weeks, and three days. I learned how to weld the summer when I was 14 years old. My father and I left my mom and three younger brothers in Levittown, Pennsylvania, where we lived in a three-bedroom house, and went to Sebree, Kentucky, population 1,558, to spend ten weeks on a welding job. Sebree had nothing but a coal mine, trailer parks, a grocery store, and a K-Mart. We welded trash cans at a small factory not far from the K-Mart. It was a hot and thankless and well-paying job that my father couldn't refuse, but he needed an extra hand and preferably a free one, so I was told, *Pack your bag, we're going to Sebree.*

I learned how to wrap a sheet of galvanized aluminum into the body of the can, hold it together with the help of a machine, and then weld down the seam, weld in the bottom circle of aluminum, and there you had it—a trash can—the big kinds you see in hospitals and schools and government buildings. We used MIG welders and my father was breaking every child labor law in the books having me there. On Saturday nights we would eat at Mack's, a local dive where we'd get heaping bowls of Kentucky chili served over spaghetti, with mounds of cheddar cheese and raw onions on top. We'd work six days a week for ten hours a day, and then on Sunday all of us on this welding job would drive across the border to Indiana and spend the day swimming and fishing in the murky waters of the Putney River, where water snakes swam right between your legs. My father and the other men would get drunk on can after can of warm Piels beer and I would drive us all back to Sebree in a big brown rusty van. It didn't matter that it was illegal for me to drive, 'cause I was among men and I was the only sober man at the end of those long Sundays. I would grip the shaky steering wheel during the drive back to Kentucky, back to the trailer park where seven of us stayed in a double-wide. They'd rotate nights on beds and sleeping bags on the floor. I never got a bed. I was reminded by the men with blackened hands and tired eyes that I was the youngest, that at my age my back—myself for that matter—could take anything.

When my father and I got home that summer, my father packed his bags again, but this time he left alone, left us all and moved to Brownfield, Maine, because he just couldn't be in a family anymore. That was what he said to my mother from a pay phone in Brattleboro, Vermont: *I can't do this anymore, Lorraine. Something's missing.*

It all runs together now, my father leaving and the summer I spent with him right before he left, living in the double-wide in Sebree and sore from the work, coffee that was bitter and scalding hot, the buzzing sound of welding, with the heat and sweat of the gear we had to wear, making trash cans so people could get rid of things and throw things away, making something to catch the unwanted, the discarded.

Howard breaking up with Daphne by e-mail was something I couldn't get out of my mind. I have trouble with technology. Janice and I don't have car phones. No DVD players. No computer. We have a VCR, but Janice is the one who deals with it. I could care less about the Internet. And e-mail—even if you aren't breaking up with someone with it—seems just altogether wrong, strange. I don't want to talk to people unless I am talking to them and seeing their mouths move as they speak or hearing the way they catch their breath or how they sound. I want to watch their eyes. Janice is patient with me about this. She wants a computer at home; she uses them at work, but she really wants one for the apartment. Janice knows I'm not ready for this stuff, that I may never be. She knew going into this marriage that I'd love her endlessly, but she knew that I'd endlessly not be easy.

I can't handle it—the technology that we can have in our homes and offices and cars and purses and back pockets—because these things move too fast for me and they all take me back to my first wife, Estelle, whom I still love, whom I can tell you right here and right now that I will never stop loving, and who is dead. Sometimes, when I'm sleeping in bed with Janice and wake up in the middle of the night with my wrist burning and my mind numb, I wonder who is next to me. I wonder.

Estelle died in a car crash, and even though I wasn't in the car, I was there. I was caught right in the middle. Estelle was talking to me on her car phone when she crashed, or when the crash occurred. We make things happen or things just happen. What's the difference?

Some of what happened will always be missing because Estelle died and the lady in the other car died and there were investigators and forensics guys and they measured tire skid marks in the road and the angle in which the cars smashed and flipped over and so there were theories, about whose fault it was, but really it doesn't matter. The whole story isn't there.

"Estelle baby, can you stop and pick up some coffee? We're out," I had said to her, hearing the sound of the radio in her 1994 blue Nissan Sentra and the swoosh of air 'cause her windows were probably half open. My last words to my wife, no wires but just air from me to her through the car phone.

"Sure thing, Turk," Estelle said. She always called me Turk, short for turkey.

"Anything else?" she asked.

But before I could answer *No,* before I could tell her that I didn't need anything else—I didn't, I had it all, I had everything I could want—came the sound. The sound like monsters screaming, metal and crunching. Nothing from Estelle. No yells, no horns, no *Oh shits* because after she asked me *Anything else?* it all was so loud and quick and then over. It was all over and then I heard the sound of traffic, of cars pulling up, of a lady who wasn't my wife screaming.

I was sitting at the kitchen table of our two-bedroom row house when Estelle died. I was there at the table but I was with her. I smelled like sweat and the two Rolling Rock beers I had quickly downed after a long day at work. I had felt too hot and lazy to get in the car and go buy coffee, and so I called Estelle. I had wanted something from her, something small. I was there, on the line, listening, waiting to come up with an answer to her question: *Anything else?*

$\sim\!\mathit{M}\!\sim$

This is what I know about Howard because of the fact that Janice and I live in the apartment above his: Howard listens to Ozzy Osbourne, Van Halen, Neil Young, Metallica. He listens to them loud, and sometimes he sings along. He doesn't sing very well. I know that Howard uses nondairy creamer in his coffee. There are always big empty Cremora containers in the recycling bin that our two apartments share. George doesn't use Cremora because at least twice last month he comes knocking on our door to borrow some milk for his coffee.

"You shouldn't be snooping like that," Janice said to me.

"I'm not snooping. Those Cremora jugs are so big you can't miss them. I swear he must go through a gallon a week."

"I thought the FDA banned that shit years ago," Janice said smiling. Janice will only drink coffee with 2 percent milk. Not half-and-half, not 1 percent, not vitamin D. It has to be 2 percent milk, with half a teaspoon of sugar.

"I guess they haven't banned it yet," I said.

"Well they should. The kid's gonna give himself cancer with that stuff," and I knew she was looking at me when she made this comment, but I didn't let myself look up at her. Because I knew what that comment was really about: Janice never lets up about my smoking and she tries to use the cancer scare tactic but I know she wants me to quit smoking because she thinks it is related to my wrist—I started smoking again when I stopped working. So if I quit smoking, she thinks it will help my wrist, which will help me get back to work, which will help us start a family. From cigarettes to babies. That's how women are. They make unconnecting things connect. Janice is 34. She has mentioned clocks ticking and ovaries shriveling up. Janice wants a house. (I sold me and Estelle's house after she died and then I gave the money to my mother-in-law, who I still visit once a month. I could not be in me and Estelle's house. I could not keep the money from the house. I couldn't. None of it.)

I know that Howard is quiet when he makes love. Sometimes I would hear Daphne, but I never heard him. I know that Howard's mother calls him every Sunday morning. His phone in his bedroom must be right under the heating vent, because warm air and Howard's voice both travel up into me and Janice's bedroom every Sunday morning. Janice is usually gone already; she works early shifts on Sundays at Luther Park, an assisted living place. She works the desk at one of the nursing stations, doing administrative stuff and answering phones and dealing with visitors; she talks all the time about going to school to become a medical transcriptionist. She tells me how the money is great, you get to work from home and make your own hours, and then when we have kids she can just work at home. On Sunday mornings I hear the sound of Howard's voice, the way he says *Mom*—not *Ma* or *Mother*, but *Mom*—and he'll stay on the phone with her for a while, mostly just listening, I suspect, because I only hear an occasional *Uh-huh,* then the steady silence until I hear nothing but his good-byes.

I was waiting for Janice to get home from work the day I saw the mug shot mug. Howard was outside on the porch, hunched over a hibachi, grilling up some turkey burgers. Howard and

George are young men with old man names, but they don't eat like men—no red meat, only turkey or chicken or fish.

"Hey, you got a Phillips head I can borrow?" I asked Howard, leaning over the railing, bits of ash from cigarette floating down so slowly I could probably catch them. I was putting together a small shelf for Janice, and I couldn't find my screwdrivers.

"Yeah, we've got a bunch somewhere. Come on down," he said.

I went downstairs and followed Harry into their apartment. Their living room was crowded by two blue couches. There was a St. Louis Rams blanket across the one couch and a framed picture of Dan Marino in his Miami Dolphins uniform on the wall. I already knew that Howard was the Rams fan and George was all about Miami.

Howard went to find the screwdrivers and I sat down at the kitchen table, which was covered with pizza coupons and bills and sports pages spread all over. On the table was a mug and one of those fancy gift bags with colored tissue paper and a card with Daphne's name on it. I picked up the mug and on it was a picture of Howard and Daphne. I had seen these at the mall before—pictures of family and wives and little babies superimposed on mugs and calendars and plaques. The picture on the mug was a face shot—a mug shot, ha!—and it said that right below the picture: *Mug Shot.* Howard and Daphne's cheeks were touching. She looked dolled up, and he was wearing this nice shirt that was silver, sort of shiny. Howard had this calm, cool, and collected smile, but she was really grinning, wide and thrilled. You could read it just in her face on the mug shot mug: This girl was in love.

I gripped the mug with my good hand, and stared at it. I hoped that Howard meant it. Putting his and this girl's picture on a mug and putting it in a pretty paper bag and giving it to a girl means something. Women take this shit seriously.

Breaking a woman's heart is something you can avoid from the get-go. Those three words should not be muttered too quickly. Not even if you are in a moment of impossible happiness, like when you see her getting out of her car and she's reaching across the seat and grabbing her sweater and headed toward you and her face breaks wide open in a smile because she sees you, she wants you. Not even if you are inside her and you are about to come and you can know no other perfect moment. Not even then.

There is no reason to tell a woman you love her unless you are going to love her forever.

<hr />

"It's wearing thin, Bob," Janice told me.

She was on her fourth beer, having worked double shifts two days in a row. She was tired, almost drunk. Janice is a good woman, smart and sensible. She doesn't complain much, hardly ever, except when things build up.

She doesn't talk anymore about buying a small house or that I'm still smoking and still not working. She doesn't have to talk about wanting babies. She doesn't even have to talk about University of Lennox, a university that doesn't have buildings or a campus, but that is on the Internet. Janice could go to school right through a computer and take courses to become a medical transcriptionist. She left the brochures on the kitchen table. We've been married for two years now and the promise is gone; the love is still there but the promise is gone, just the reality, the commitment, the daily grind, and now she's living with me, with my way, with quiet and no wires humming or bright screens. No access.

"I know, baby. It's wearing thin for me, too, but it'll be okay soon," I said.

"They still can't find anything wrong with your wrist. I don't understand why you still have so much pain," she said, not even looking up at me.

"Today the doctor said if things aren't better in another month, he's sending me to this specialist in Washington, D.C."

"Really?"

"Yeah, baby. This guy in D.C. gets people back to work in weeks. I'm getting to the bottom of all of this, I promise."

I told Janice this lie because she wanted to know that everything will be okay. I hadn't even seen a real doctor that day. I had seen a technician. I had gone to a clinic for neuropsychological tests. The people who cut my disability checks told me I had to go. The technician was a young woman with wide white teeth and perfect lips who ran test after test after test.

"Maybe it's from my cat," I joked to the technician.

"I'm sorry, Mr. Pyrah, I don't think I understand," she said. She looked up from her chart, a piece of her long black hair falling onto her cheek, sliding toward her mouth. The same piece of hair kept falling to her face the whole time I was there, and she kept pushing it back.

"I walk my cat. Maybe it's from him." I said.

"I still don't understand, I'm sorry," she said, looking worried, lightly shaking her head but grinning the kind of grin that is meant to be a polite *I'm sorry*.

"I walk my cat on a leash. He's practically like a dog, and he likes to be walked around outside on a leash. Maybe he pulls too hard? You know? Maybe that's the whole wrist thing?" I said, still just trying to joke with her.

Her nervous grin disappeared and a relaxed one took its place.

"It'd have to be a mighty big cat, Mr. Pyrah," and she went back to her chart, back to asking me questions, making notes, conducting tests, making sure my pain was real.

A girl came to Howard and George's apartment in the middle of the day about a week after Howard told George it was over with Daphne. It was Wednesday. It was 2 PM. I wasn't used to seeing people in the middle of the day; it was as if the middle of the day was only mine.

She didn't notice me on the balcony as she came across the walkway. I was ready to light a cigarette, and when I saw her I stopped, held my breath, didn't move. She was wearing a pair of blue jeans, black flip-flops, and a gray shirt that just scraped the top of her pants—revealing the smallest amount of the skin of her belly. I lost sight of her when she was directly under the balcony at Howard and George's door, but I didn't hear her knock or ring a bell. I lit my cigarette. And then I saw her again, walking away. She was a breath, not even two puffs on my cigarette.

I had no choice: I went downstairs to Howard and George's apartment to see. I had to—because of all that I knew and that I did not know, because I had seen the mug shot mug, because of what it feels like to not work all day. How time moves in this breath-holding slow time, how you are curious about the rest of the world and what they are doing and how they feel because there is nothing left that you feel. Nothing but the pain in your wrist, so you are looking to other people and what they are doing and feeling, because all you feel is this pit-of-your-stomach sense that something is missing.

I went to Howard and George's apartment and taped to their door was a piece of paper. A girl had shown up, *shown up,* not by e-mail, not by regular mail, not by anything else but in person—live and in the flesh. I took the piece of paper taped to the door, folded it into a small square and put it in my pocket. I went back to me and Janice's apartment, went outside on our balcony and I took out another cigarette and I lit it and I took the paper out, inhaled deep. Poems. It said *From Friends of Daphne* at the top of the paper.

Ode to the Spineless

Howard, Howard, six months of bliss
Then you leave without a kiss.
Why did you put the picture on the mug?
We thought Cupid your heart did tug.
Howard, you laid it on real thick
To withdraw your affection so quick.
And to end it all by electronic mail
Is the ultimate spineless way to bail.
But fret not, Howard—take your place in line
With the other guys who now do pine.
In several weeks you'll realize your error.
And Daphne will be off in fields a-fairer.

A Rhyme for the Electronic Dumper

You nice-guy-looking thug!
You put that picture on a mug!
In your shiny shirt, like John Travolta
To all Daphne's friends you're known as
    "Howard Revolt-a"
So kiss off you lame and pathetic Howard,
Cause dumping a woman by e-mail makes you a
    fucking coward.

I once read an article about e-mail. It was about how the messages actually physically move, how your love note or directions to your cookout or office memo are transmitted through the wires, how the e-mail is broken up into a kazillion little pieces, like a puzzle. How the computer takes the e-mail message and pulverizes it, crashes and burns it into countless tiny pieces and then sends these puzzle pieces flying through the wires. And when these tiny pieces of information arrive on the other end, to their destination, another computer figures it all out and puts all the pieces of the puzzle together.

The next day, in the early evening, I was outside on the balcony. Janice was still at work. I saw Howard walking backward on the lawn, looking up at me sitting on my balcony.

"Hey, Bob, I've got a package of yours down here."

"I didn't order anything." I wasn't much in the mood to chat with anyone, especially with Howard. Howard the Coward, I kept thinking. I'm Bad Ass Bob and he's Howard the Coward.

"Well, it's got Janice's name on it," Howard said, still being nice, still clueless.

"Well then I guess Janice ordered something," I said sarcastically.

"Well, you're gonna need help carrying it upstairs—you know with your hand and all—so is it okay if I bring it upstairs?"

"It's my wrist," I said.

"Excuse me?"

"My wrist. It's my wrist. My hand is fine. It's all in the wrist."

"Yeah," Howard said, "that's what my tennis coach used to say to me in high school. *It's all in the wrist.*" Howard cracked a smile but I wasn't laughing. Everything was wearing thin, like Janice said.

I walked down to Howard and George's patio and on it were two huge boxes and one small one. It said MacIntosh everywhere across it.

"This is one sweet piece of machinery, Bob. It's got more speed than you'll ever need. And it looks like Janice picked out a cute color too," he said, giving me a playful wink.

Fuck you, Howard, I thought. *Just totally fuck you.*

My wife was moving everything faster, past me, toward everything that would come next and here was Howard to help; here he was offering his brute force, his physical presence, his strong back and willingness and offer to take this upstairs.

I carried the box that held the keyboard, and I pretended it was okay that I was carrying this little lightweight box while

Howard lugged up the heavier boxes. I had to be silent and this is what I swallowed: *Leave all of it on the patio because it is all going back because that was a dumb fucking move on my wife's part. You don't know, Howard. You do not have a second wife. You do not have a dead first wife. You do not even know how to break up with a woman, you sad little fuck, acting all big, carrying heavy boxes.*

Janice came home and the computer was sitting on the living room floor, the boxes unopened. She was going to be a medical transcriptionist. There was no fight. No need for it. Nothing to say. I said nothing and she said nothing and Janice got her way.

She had always been a tough bird, and maybe the bird was just done with my way and was getting ready to fly her way.

⁓

I go outside to walk Boots, and Howard is on the grass stretching, getting ready to go for a run.

It has been one week since I found the poems Daphne's friends left for him, the poems he doesn't even know are missing. It has been six days since the computer arrived, six days since I've spoken a single word to my wife.

"Hey, Bob," Howard says, sounding cheerful and upbeat. "How goes it?"

"It goes, Howard, you know. It goes."

Howard is standing up, holding his left leg bent behind him, holding it by the ankle, making it stretch.

"So how's that new computer running?" he asks, not knowing a fucking thing.

"Quickly, Howard. It all runs so quickly. How about you? How's that girl of yours? Haven't seen her around much lately," I say sarcastically, diving right in, not wasting time. Moving with the fast pace, trying to catch up.

We break up with women and ruin relationships and bring things to their end for reasons that make sense—because they complain too much, because they constantly pick fights, because they get fat, because the relationship has been going on forever and it appears that forever is going nowhere and you know you just are never gonna love the girl even though you really thought you could; because of how much she seems to not need you at all or way too much; because of her mother. And we bring things to an end for reasons that don't make sense—because that strange moan she gives out when you make love to her, that moan that you liked so much, that was so *her* when you first made love to her now annoys you, freaks you out, scares you, makes you wonder what kind of animal you are inside of; because her teeth are too small. But no matter how small the story, no matter how poor the excuse, we must be men about it. We can be lousy crappy small men, but we must still be men.

"We're not involved anymore," he says.

"Not involved?" I ask, pushing.

"We broke up," he says, looking defensive.

"Breaking up is hard to do."

"You said it," he says, starting to look annoyed.

"No, Neil Sedaka said it," and I crack a huge grin and break into song. *Breaking up is hard to do-hoo-hoooo-hoo*. I am grinning at Howard. Smiling wide.

"Whatever. Listen I'll catch you later," he says, getting ready to put his Sports Walkman on his ears.

"Wait a second," I say and I touch Howard's shoulder.

Howard looks scared. He doesn't know what isn't right, but he knows something isn't right. His nostrils flare out.

"Were you a man about it?"

"What the fuck?" Howard asks, now pissed.

"Well? Were you?"

"Fuck you, Bob," he spits.

That's better, I think. *Things are getting better,* I think. *My wife and I have not spoken in six days, but it will be okay,* I think.

"Well?" I ask, feeling warm and red in the face. I want an answer.

"Just get the fuck out of here," he says and he is not walking away, he is not backing down.

I stand there looking at him. It is 6 PM in May and my wife, Janice, is at work getting ready to come home from her job where she will turn on the new computer I did not want and move her life, maybe our life, onward and faster and toward something that is not here yet, and you can smell autumn olive in the air and Howard is going to go for a run and we are standing there face to face. I have let go of the leash and Boots, unaware of his freedom, of his right to just move on, has not drifted very far.

"Well, were you a man about it?" I ask again.

"Bob, you better get the fuck out of here," he says, and he starts to shake his right hand. (My wrist tingles; it doesn't hurt, it tingles.) Howard is shaking his right hand, like he's warming it up, loosening his wrist, getting ready.

"Were you a man about it or not?" I ask and Howard breaks. Like a fault line. And I can see the man coming out. He steps back, because he is going to move forward. That is how it works: a step back to bring it forward and I see his right hand, the one he has been shaking, being drawn back, his arm moving back, bending at the elbow.

And I meet him and he meets me and our bodies have joined—his fist, my face, and blood comes down my nose. I grin at him, at the scared look on his face.

It is scary becoming a man.

I walk away. Howard is standing there silent, my blood on his hands, and I go get Boots, who has drifted across the apartment complex lawn. I pick Boots up and he looks up at me, his whiskers looking saggy. Boots is getting old, not long for the day.

I know that Janice will be home soon. I wish she was home now. When she gets home I'm going to make love to her. Nothing in my wrist burns right now. There is no pain. Janice will be home soon and I will hold her close. I will hold my beautiful wife close to my body and I will make love to her. I want to make sweet sweet love to my wife Janice and I want to make a baby with her, tonight, a son, we'll make a son. I am going to love my wife with everything I have. With absolutely everything. With all of it.

Printed in the United States
by Baker & Taylor Publisher Services